Leaving Laos

May Y. Yang

<u>Disclaimer</u>

This book is a work of fiction. Although set in a historical context, names of places and chronology of events have been changed or rearranged for the convenience of narration. Apart from public figures, all the characters are fictitious. The opinions expressed in the story are that of the characters for plot development and are not that of the author.

Cover Illustration by Xia Thao

ISBN-10: 1981229310
ISBN-13: 9781981229314

For my husband Nhia Xue Yang.
After all these years, the spell has not broken. I hope it never does. I am uplifted by your love, devotion, and affection. I love my life with you.

To my beloved mother Shoua Vang.
I still remember the story you told about going to work at the farm and feeling overwhelmed with emptiness, for it seemed like the entire world had left Laos. That feeling that you described is one of the inspirations for this book.

To my children Nathan, Gregory, Athena, and Brandon.
You are my joy and my blessings. I am one lucky mama!

Chapter 1

I am thinking of Laos again. I think of Laos often, especially when the weather here in Minnesota starts to turn chilly in autumn. I think of the green of the plants in the rainy season and the early morning mists that rose to block my view of the mountains in the distance. I think of rice fields and a narrow dirt path leading to a tiny, ramshackle hut. I think of two children riding a bike along a desolate road, the second child with his arms spread out as if he were flying.

I long for the heat and humidity of Laos all through winter when the snow in Minnesota is thick, and the frigid air penetrates through my layers of clothing, making me want to curl up indoors until spring. I think of Laos in early spring, when all the leaves, flowers, and grass are trying to peek out from under the lingering cold that is doggedly pushing back the coming of warm weather.

I think of Laos when I hear a Hmong song, so many of which express the hope for things to become better back home so that we can return to visit those who stayed behind. Some of the young singers have never been to Laos; and some, like me, left Laos when they were children. They sing the words perfectly, but when they speak, they switch back and forth between English and Hmong. I, too, am forgetting certain Hmong words and frequently use English even when talking with an elder. My girlfriend's father complains about my generation losing our Hmong language. I am embarrassed to say that I have tried to carry an entire conversation with him in Hmong to impress him, but I have failed miserably every time.

Memories of Laos hit me hardest every Hmong New Year when parents loosen their tight budgets to buy the perfect New Year's clothes for their children and plenty of food for the New Year's festivities. When my grandma and aunts set out large aluminum trays of food, and relatives arrive with even more food than we can possibly eat in a day, I find myself thinking about my sister and the little food and possessions we had growing up.

When Grandma or Aunt Jer presses a hard-boiled egg that has been blessed by a shaman in celebration of the upcoming New Year into my hand, I wish I could offer one to my sister. In many dreams, my sister and I are reunited. She is here with me, and we talk eagerly about how many years have passed and how much we have missed each other. But I always wake up to disappointment. I haven't seen her in over seven years. My communication with her has been through letters, audiocassettes, and two phone calls over a line crackling with static.

As I walk across the Washington Avenue Bridge over the calm Mississippi River to the West Bank campus to my early morning class, I think of my sister back in the refugee camp in Thailand. Once I graduate and get a well-paying job and my own place, I'm going to bring her and her family here. She'll be so amazed when she sees Minnesota. It's nothing like the refugee camp. I hope she will be proud of me.

I long to share a meal with her as an adult. If she ever comes, my table will be laden with all she has ever wanted, hinted at, or merely mentioned as something she noticed at the market. At every Hmong gathering, the tables are full. It is our custom to invite guests to eat and have seconds and thirds and so on. But more than that, this one small gesture will be my way of saying to her that I love her, and I thank her for being everything a person can be in a family to a small orphaned boy.

Most Americans have heard about the Vietnam War. But what most Americans don't know is that the war didn't just stay in Vietnam. It spilled over into the neighboring country of Laos. The Communist Pathet Lao was fighting to overthrow the Royal Lao Government, just like the Communist Viet Cong was trying to overthrow the South Vietnamese government and unify North Vietnam with South Vietnam. The Communist Pathet Lao saw themselves as trying to liberate Laos from the control and influences of the French. Therefore, they sympathized with the Communist Viet Cong and North Vietnam, whom they saw as trying to do the same thing in South Vietnam.

How tragic that in attempting to push out foreign control, members of the Lao Royal Family allowed foreign forces to divide them. This led to the end of the Lao monarchy, which had existed for over six hundred years. The Communist Pathet Lao, led by Prince Souphanouvong, who was a distant cousin of the king and also nicknamed the Red Prince, forced King Savang Vatthana to abdicate the throne in 1975.

A framed photo of King Savang Vatthana and Queen Khamphoui, taken during happier times, still hangs on a wall in our living room along with an aerial photo of Long Cheng airbase. In the picture, the King and Queen are sitting next to each other. The King is leaning towards the Queen as if in a private conversation. They are an attractive couple. They look dignified and happy. Who could have predicted that they were going to be arrested and sent to die in a re-education camp?

At that time America was afraid of the spread of Communism. It believed that if one country in Southeast Asia fell to Communism, the rest would follow, creating a domino effect. It was that fear that allowed America to be influenced by France to interfere in the civil war in Vietnam, which also led to America's involvement in Laos.

When the American government needed help fighting the North Vietnamese forces that were coming into northern Laos as well as the Communist threats that were developing inside Laos, they recruited the Hmong, a small ethnic group in northern Laos. The United States CIA enlisted the help of

General Vang Pao, a high-ranking Hmong official in the Royal Lao Army, to form an army to fight against the Communists.

However, Laos was not officially involved in the Vietnam War, so the CIA had to keep their activities in Laos a secret. The North Vietnamese was also supplying the Viet Cong in South Vietnam. The supply line, known as the Ho Chi Minh Trail, ran along the western borders of North Vietnam and South Vietnam, and parts of the trail crossed into Laos. The CIA wanted to stop this supply line.

For years and years, American bombs dropped on the countryside of Laos. Some of those bombs did not explode, and tragically, to this day the people of Laos, especially young children or farmers clearing land, are sometimes killed or maimed by exploding bombs. While American airmen dropped bombs on Laos, young Hmong men, even boys as young as 13, were recruited as foot soldiers to fight the Communist and rescue American pilots when their planes were shot down. The United States government kept it all a secret. They called it a Secret War. But it was no secret to us.

Chapter 2

The year was 1975. I was without a father and a mother. We were living in Long Cheng. According to my grandpa's calculations, I must have been about eleven or twelve years old. Of course, his calculations were based on the season in which I was born and the events of each year since my birth. For a long time, the Hmong people did not have a written language, and even after a written language was created, many Hmong did not have an opportunity to learn to read and write, so most Hmong did not keep records of birth dates.

My sister Ka-Ying and I were living with our father's family, which included our grandparents; my father's younger brother Kou and his wife; and my father's youngest brother Jer, who was at that time away at school in the capital city of Vientiane. My father's oldest brother Lue and his wife had lived with us, but several years after my father passed away, they moved to Na Su to be closer to Aunt Lue's family. Grandma had only one daughter, and she was my kind Aunt Pahoua, who lived in Vientiane with her family. She was beloved by everyone we knew, and her visits always called for a small celebration.

At the time of my father's death, I was about a year old. My mother remarried when I was around two. When I became older, my mother told me that she had to remarry because life was difficult for a young widow. She didn't want to be a burden to my father's family. I didn't think my father's family would consider her a burden, but I never wanted to talk with her about why she remarried. Since I was a boy, I could not go with her. I had to stay with my father's side of the family to carry on his name. Because I was still a

5

toddler at the time, my sister Ka-Ying, who was five or six, stayed to help care for me.

Ka-Ying became my father, mother, and best friend. She was the one who beamed with pride when I accomplished a little task. She was the one who squatted down in front of me to wipe my scraped knee when I fell. She was the one I secretly cried to when I missed my mother. She also told me stories about my father, whom I was too young to remember. She showed me how he used to spring out of bed like a Chinese kung fu star, kicking his feet under him and pushing off with his hands behind his head. I used to practice that move over and over, imagining I would be just like my dad.

Long Cheng was a secret military base set up by the United States CIA, high in the mountains of Laos. Almost every man who lived there worked for the Americans. Most were foot soldiers and pilots, but some worked in the hospital. Some women worked for the CIA too, mostly in the hospital, but a few worked with men at the military radio station. My father, Uncle Lue, and Uncle Kou worked as soldiers. After my father passed away, my grandpa became bitter and angry. Not only did he lose my father, his second-eldest son, but he also never had the chance to give my father a funeral and burial.

As far back as I could remember, we had made Long Cheng our home. And war was a constant part of our lives. We sometimes had to move to other villages for a few months, but we always returned to Long Cheng and resumed our lives. My grandmother and aunts would go out to the fields every morning before the sun was high to farm and pick vegetables. Uncle Kou proudly drove his motorcycle every morning to the military base. Several days a week Ka-Ying and I went to the market with Grandma to sell vegetables. Some afternoons I played with my friend Pao while my sister helped prepare the evening meal of rice, boiled or stir-fried vegetables, and pepper paste.

Grandpa had a small radio that he carried everywhere he went. He liked listening to the news on the radio and became the ear to the world for our family and friends and neighbors. Every day he would tell us things that were happening in Laos and in strange-sounding, faraway places.

One morning I found Grandpa listening to the radio like he always did, but he was shaking his head as he was listening to it. He had the radio close to his ear.

"Grandpa, what's going on?" I asked.

He did not answer me. Grandma had told me that Grandpa was becoming deaf from listening to the radio. Sometimes he even went to bed holding the radio next to his ear. I asked him again, but louder, "Grandpa, what's going on?"

"I heard you the first time. Go away!" he barked.

I walked out the back door feeling upset and uneasy. Then I heard the sound of a motorcycle roaring up the dirt road from the valley below. It was my Uncle Kou. I wondered why he was home early. I sat down on the wooden bench by the back door and looked down on the village and the airplanes landing and taking off. I heard the motorcycle rumble to a stop at the front of the house and then my uncle's voice shouting, "Dad, where are you?"

I went inside to see my uncle standing before Grandpa, who was still holding the radio but not close to his ear anymore.

"Dad, the war is over! The Americans are pulling out." Uncle Kou announced breathlessly. It was unlike my uncle to ever be breathless when talking about anything. "It is too dangerous for us to stay now. If the Communists find out that I worked for the Americans—" He stopped and shook his head. "Tomorrow there will be airplanes to take us to Thailand. We must leave Laos!"

"Tomorrow?" Grandpa replied in disbelief. "What about our relatives—my brothers, your uncles? I need to let them know and find out if they want to go with us!"

7

These relatives lived in other villages. It would be a day's journey to reach some of them. Because they were far from Long Cheng, they might not even know that the war was over.

"We don't have time for that!" my uncle exclaimed sharply. "Tomorrow is the only day the airplanes will be provided by the Americans. We need to be there early so that we can be the first ones in line to board the planes."

Grandpa vehemently shook his head no. The decision was too big. He needed time to think. He seemed at a complete loss.

"Dad, you know how much some Laotians hate the Hmong," Uncle Kou said. "Well, the Communists despise us even more! We must flee to Thailand."

Grandpa crumpled onto a low stool. He sat with his head in his hands. My dad had already died in the war, and I guess Grandpa did not want to see any more of his sons killed. Grandpa must have sensed too that the Communist Pathet Lao's victory was going to forever change Laos.

"Blong, why don't you go and catch two chickens, so we can butcher them for lunch," Grandpa said suddenly.

"You mean one chicken, right, Grandpa?" I asked.

"No! Two! Make sure they are big ones," ordered Grandpa.

I could hardly believe what Grandpa had just said. Usually, we would butcher only one or two chickens in a month, and only if we were feeling indulgent, celebrating a special occasion, or hosting important guests. Now we were going to eat two chickens for lunch. I hurried off to catch chickens in case Grandpa changed his mind.

That evening we also butchered a pig that we had been saving for the upcoming New Year's feast. We invited close friends and neighbors to enjoy our last meal with us. There was a heaviness in the air. The adults talked of many things. Some of the guests said they would be fleeing Laos too. Others said they would stay behind and see what

8

develops. They hoped that the Communists would allow the Hmong to carry on with their lives as before. The adults moved from talks of goodbye to talks of reuniting in the near future. Uncertainty hung in the air.

That meal was the first time I could have as much meat as I wanted without anyone saying something to me or giving me disapproving looks. I even got another chicken drumstick. That was two in one day, which had never happened before. Drumsticks were usually given to a favorite child or a special person, which meant if my cousins Tong and Lia were visiting, their mother would make sure they got the drumsticks. Still, I couldn't really enjoy the food, thinking about what tomorrow might bring. I had never been on an airplane. I had never been to Thailand. What did it all mean? After dinner, we packed up some leftover food for our guests and said farewell to them.

Chapter 3

I went outside to wash my greasy hands and face with water from the large metal drum that we used as a rain barrel. At one time the army had used it to transport gasoline, but we now used it to collect and store water. The metal drum sat at the corner of the house, under the bamboo pipes that served as gutters to direct rainwater from the roof into the drum.

My sister approached me, and I could hear her sobs as she tried to stifle them. She was wiping her tears with the back of her hand. I wondered what Aunt Kou had said this time to make her cry. Uncle Kou's wife had her own name, but I never knew what it was. In keeping with Hmong custom, my sister and I called her by our uncle's name. Aunt and Uncle Kou had been married for almost a year, and now she was pregnant with their first child. She had been quiet and soft-spoken, but now the pregnancy or the restlessness of war was making her short-tempered. Sometimes she snapped at my sister for minor things.

"Mom wants to see you," Ka-Ying said through her tears.

"Where is she?" I asked. My mother lived with her husband and her two new children on the other side of town. Usually, if I did not go visit her, I would not see her because she rarely came to our side of town.

"She's in the front yard," Ka-Ying replied.

I followed Ka-Ying to the front of the house. As I turned the corner, I saw my mother standing just outside the front door. I guessed no adult in the family had seen her, so no one had invited her inside. Her back was to the front door, and I saw her in profile as I approached. She seemed to be looking far away, off into the peaks of the surrounding mountains. A breeze blew at her yellow Laotian sarong, making the skirt flutter about her ankles. She looked young—too young to be a mother of four—and immeasurably sad and vulnerable. I thought to myself that if the breeze picked up, she might tumble away with it. She must have seen or heard us approaching, for she turned to us expectantly. She did not say hello, and I did not greet her either. We simply began talking, as if we still lived in one house, as if we were still one family unit. To say hello would have seemed too formal. It would have meant acknowledging that there was some distance between us.

"Your stepdad Nukee and I are not leaving," my mother said. "I want you and your sister to stay together."

I nodded. Of course, my sister would go with me. It had never occurred to me that it could be otherwise. Although no one had ever told me so, I knew that Ka-Ying could have gone to live with my mother and her new family anytime. She could have had a mother to teach her. She could have had all the things that a young teenage girl needed and wanted. Instead, she had chosen to stay and take care of me. As far as I knew, that's how it would always remain.

"You have to listen to your sister," my mother continued. "She is older than you, but you must protect her. You are her brother."

"I know, Mom. We have been on our own for a long time now. We know what to do." I tried to sound strong and grown-up. I wanted to remove the worry from her eyes.

"No matter where you and your sister go, I will find out and stay in touch. I may not be there to help both of you, but I will stay in touch." She paused and stared off toward the mountaintops again. I just stood there and watched her. When she turned to me again, her eyes were brimming with tears, but she did not cry out loud, and she did not sob. "I know things have been difficult. If I could have done it, I would have taken you both to live with me a long time ago. I took comfort in the fact that at least we lived in the same town. Now, it seems like everyone is talking about fleeing to

11

Thailand. Your uncle and grandparents are taking you and Ka-Ying. We might never see one another again. I gave your sister some money to share with you. Please be helpful and obedient and always take good care of each other."

For the first time, I realized what it all meant. We were really going to leave, and I might never see my mother again.

For so long I had been angry with my mother because she had left my sister and me to start a new family. She now had two little girls with her new husband. Whenever Ka-Ying and I visited my mother, her new daughters called me big brother and Ka-Ying big sister. They eagerly talked to us and shared treats such as sugarcane or pieces of candy. But our visits were infrequent, and we never stayed overnight. I always ended up missing my grandpa. I was afraid he might be lonesome or missing me. Because I did not want to spend the night, Ka-Ying never slept over either. A tiny part of me was afraid that Ka-Ying might decide to go live with them so that she could have sisters. I was secretly glad that Ka-Ying always came home with me.

My half-sisters were kind and polite, but a part of me was sometimes jealous of them whenever I saw how my mother doted on them. Sometimes when Ka-Ying and I had to work extra hard or when we were yelled at by our grandparents or uncles and aunts, I found myself becoming resentful of my mother. I would be so upset that on days when I was allowed to go visit her, I chose not to, just to punish her. Now, I tried to think of an angry thought so that I would not cry, but against my will, my eyes filled with tears. I turned away from her, hoping she would not know I was crying.

Then I felt my mother's hands on my shoulders, and as I turned around, she pulled me into her arms. So much for my toughness. I pressed my cheek against her and wrapped my arms around her waist. It felt comforting to have a mother to bury my face against. I gave in to my sobs and hugged her tightly as I cried. She extended one arm to invite my sister into her embrace. The three of us held tightly to one another as we cried. It was a farewell embrace and a mother's embrace. My sister and I were rarely held by an adult like that. It felt soothing, satisfying, and heartbreaking all at the same time. I had forgotten how good it felt to be in my mother's arms, and I did not want to let her go.

"Ka-Ying! Blong! Come pack your things!" Uncle Kou shouted from within the house.

"Yes, Uncle!" Ka-Ying called back but made no movement to go inside.

Either because he was annoyed by my sister's inaction or curious about the note of tears in her voice, Uncle Kou stuck his head out the door to see what was going on. He looked surprised to see my mother there.

"Oh! Hello, sister-in-law. Come inside," invited Uncle Kou.

"I was about to leave," my mother said. She paused for a moment and wiped her tears. As she looked up at my uncle in the doorway, I wondered if she was thinking about how this house had once been her home. She and her husband, my father, had chosen this spot, about halfway up on the mountain, a perfect location. When it was New Year, they could look down and see the entire field below filled with people wearing new, beautiful, and colorful clothes to celebrate the New Year festivities.

My mother had told me how they built their house. They used wood from trees that my father chopped down and metal from fuel drums discarded by the Americans. Steel was more durable than bamboo, as it resisted weathering. It made good roofing and siding for the walls and would not rot and need replacing. But it was grueling work. My father had to cut through the metal drums with a hand saw and pound on the curved metal to flatten it. She begged him to stop because of the blisters and cuts on his hands, but he told her he wanted to make their house last for their children and grandchildren.

Once the house was finished, they tilled up the land around it. On the east side of the house, they planted pineapple plants, and on the west side, banana trees, mango trees, orange trees, passion fruit vines, and herbs. The herb garden had been my mother's idea. Every young wife wanted an herb garden nearby so that she could step outside to pick a few leaves to season her cooking, but it was my father who tended and watered the plants so that she could enjoy such a garden.

My mother once said that Aunt Lue had teasingly called her spoiled because my father's older brother, Uncle Lue, would not do the same thing for Aunt Lue. "Lue makes me fetch firewood when it is cold outside, and you—your husband not only fetches the firewood by himself, but he even starts the fire for you!" Mom said Aunt Lue tried to make her words sound like banter, but the words flew out like accusations.

My mother and father lived for a little over a year in their new home, and then my father was killed fighting in the war. His body was never recovered. His good friend, who survived, said the enemy fire was intense. With tears in his eyes, he said he saw my father being shot at and die, but he could not reach him to bring him home. My mother sometimes cried that she did not even get the chance to tend to my father's corpse and give him a burial.

"Uncle Kou," she said, addressing him in the same way her own children called him. "You help look after Blong and Ka-Ying." She looked like she wanted to say more to him, perhaps remind him of how kind her husband was to him and that he owed it to her husband to be extra kind to her children, but it was not her place anymore. She was no longer a part of the family.

"I'll look after them as if they were my own children," Uncle Kou promised.

14

My mother looked at Uncle Kou as if she did not believe him. Uncle Kou did not have any children of his own yet. And my mother knew, because we had told her, that Uncle Kou sometimes unfairly reprimanded and yelled at us. He could be overly critical and rageful and often had harsh words for Ka-Ying. Mom herself had told us many times how different Uncle Kou's personality was from our father's gentle nature.

"Sister-in-law, don't worry about your children. As long as I am alive, I will take care of them." As if anxious to reassure her, he added, "Come in, please."

My mother glanced past him through the doorway. She must have known that it was an empty invitation; the house was no longer one for receiving guests. Our meager possessions were mostly packed up.

"No, thank you, brother-in-law. I must go now," she said. She gently patted my sister's head and mine and then turned to depart. Uncle Kou went back inside the house. Ka-Ying and I remained standing and watched her walk away. She had her own family to take care of; her two little girls were waiting for her. A few paces away, Mom stopped to glance back at us. She was not that far away yet, and I could see tears glistening on her cheeks. Ka-Ying pulled me closer to her and held me as we watched until our mother disappeared behind the thick grove of banana trees.

Chapter 4

We were one of the first families to arrive at the airport, which was really no airport but a strip of land that military planes used for landing and taking off. We thought we would be among the first group to get on the plane, but no, not us. As more and more people arrived and there was no plane in sight, one of the Hmong organizers got out a megaphone and shouted for all of us to get into groups according to our clan. When the plane arrived, each group would board with its clan leader, he explained.

We looked for and slowly moved toward our clan leader. He did not have a high rank in the local government, so we were pushed farther and farther to the back of the line. Uncle Kou tried to get us closer to the front, but in every group that we approached, old friends and neighbors did not seem to notice or remember my uncle and grandpa. Uncle Kou was visibly angry.

"Look at these so-called friends! Look at how easily they forget all the favors I did for them!" Uncle Kou spat. He directed his words toward Grandpa, but I knew he deliberately raised his voice to be sure everyone else could hear him. Still frustrated, Uncle Kou told us to stay where we were. Then he wheeled around and stalked away.

"Where are you going?" Grandpa yelled after him.

"Stay with the group! I am going to see a friend. I'll be back!" Uncle Kou called out before disappearing into the crowd.

I looked around and saw my best friend Pao. He was there too with his prized rooster. There were several other boys with him. Just the other day, we had held a rooster fight, with my rooster winning out over his. I was surprised he still had his rooster. I thought for certain his mother would have made him leave it behind.

"Hey, Pao!" I called as I ran toward him.

"Where is your rooster?" he asked me.

"My grandpa said we could not take a rooster with us on the plane, so I had to leave it behind," I told him.

"My father said the same thing too, but I begged, so he let me keep it," Pao said proudly.

"I didn't do that," I said, shaking my head for emphasis. "Grandpa was firm about me not taking the rooster. I didn't want to make him angry."

Pao looked at me skeptically. But I wasn't lying. Grandpa was agitated and grumpy about us packing and coming to the airport. I knew better than to whine when Grandpa had already told me not to bring my rooster.

Pao introduced me to the other boys and then resumed a story he was telling. About an hour passed. There were no airplanes in sight. People were becoming impatient and restless. Many sat on their bundles and suitcases. I did not mind the wait, however, because I was having fun playing with Pao and the new friends I had just met. After a while I heard my sister calling me.

"Blong! There you are!" she shouted, yanking me up by the arm. "Why didn't you answer me? You were not supposed to wander this far off! Grandpa is really mad at you," my sister warned me as I followed her back to our group.

Sometimes Grandpa would have such a bad temper, especially when he was drunk. Everybody hated him when he was drunk, including me. But when I was younger, he was the one who carried me on his back in the middle of the night when we had to run for shelter during an air raid. He always took care of me even when he was frustrated with me or with something else.

"Where did you go?" Grandpa demanded. I noticed that we had been pushed all the way to the back of the line. I wondered if it was my fault.

"I was with Pao, just over there." I pointed to the spot to let him know that I did not wander far, even though I knew that with all these people, there was no way he could have found me if there had been an emergency.

"Come on, let's go!" Uncle Kou interrupted. "Captain Yang Cher said we could join his group."

We picked up our bundles and followed my uncle. We probably moved up ten or twelve groups. My uncle was happy and told us that we had a better chance now of boarding a plane.

It was around noon when the first airplane arrived, a huge military cargo jet. It landed and slowly taxied toward the waiting crowd. As it came closer, the force of the wind from the propeller blew so strong and so loud that I could feel my skin vibrating. My black felt cap flew off my head.

The tail of the airplane was wide. It looked like a huge duck tail. As the plane slowed, a door opened from under the tail and became a ramp. The people around us grabbed their belongings and the hand of a child or an elder. Some people held on to their things because they were afraid their things might fly away due to the wind of the airplane. Other people held on to their things in preparation to climb up the ramp.

The moment the airplane came to a complete stop, people started running toward it and climbing up the ramp. All the rules about boarding by groups were disregarded. The people who were going to follow the rules were caught by surprise. They just stood there with their mouths opened, confused about the chaos. We watched in disbelief. By the time we realized what was happening, the airplane was already past capacity. The ramp started to close as the airplane pulled away. Americans on the plane gestured for people not to climb on anymore. The plane was crowded, and the ramp needed to close.

The people who were left behind became angry and scared. They stared nervously at the sky, watching for other planes to appear. Soon another cargo plane arrived. As it started to descend, the crowd got ready to spring into action. They were determined not to be left behind again. The plane landed, and people started running after it even though it had not come to a standstill. As the plane turned, the people chasing the plane also turned, as if they were connected to it, falling and tumbling behind like cans tied to a newlywed couple's car. When the airplane's back door began to open, people started jumping and scrambling onto the ramp.

The same thing happened with another plane, and then another. Out of panic, fear, and frustration, people were endangering their lives by chasing after the planes and jumping onto the ramps before they were fully lowered. The situation also made it hard for the pilot, crew, and the government officials who were trying to organize the evacuation. Finally, the officials got smart.

"Attention!" an official called out through a megaphone. "The Communists are getting ready to bomb the area! Please seek shelter immediately!"

My sister snatched my hand, and we ran toward the foothills, hardly daring to look up at the sky, where we were certain the bombers would be appearing at any moment. When we and the other people who ran reached the foothills, we looked back and saw that many people, including the officials and their families, had not dispersed or sought shelter. They remained where they were. They were in danger of being killed.

"Why aren't they taking cover? Those fools!" someone shouted.

Then we saw it. The plane was not a bomber but another cargo plane. It had touched down and was slowly moving towards the crowd. We were the fools! We ran back from the foothills as fast as we could, but most of the officials' families were now boarding the plane. Tempers flared. I felt pushed forward in the crush of the people and was almost knocked down as loud voices shouted near my ear. Up ahead, people started to argue. Someone even pulled out a gun. The American workers got scared, closed the door, and yelled for the pilot to pull out. People started running after the plane, hanging on to the door. Some people managed to get inside the plane before the door closed, but some fell off the plane as it taxied down the runway.

After that, there were no more planes. We waited and waited, but there was no sound of an airplane approaching. We looked around in disbelief. The sky looked gray and empty. There was not a single bird in the sky to give us a false hope that it could transform into an airplane. We watched the others as they picked up their bundles and walked away from the airport. They disappeared behind buildings and clusters of trees to reappear on the slopes of the surrounding mountains, each of them going back to what was considered home even if their hearts had already left on the planes, soaring across the sky out of Laos and into Thailand.

As I stood in the middle of the airfield and watched the people walking up the paths of those mountains, I wondered if they still had homes, livestock, and other possessions waiting for them, or whether they, like us, had given everything away, thinking they were going to leave Laos forever.

We did not want to return home yet. We stayed at the airport and hoped that another airplane would emerge from the overcast sky. Maybe this time we would be able to get on, we thought, because there were not many people left still waiting; but a plane never came. There were no more planes leaving Laos. All our leaders had abandoned us. This military base that had once buzzed nonstop with the sounds of planes, automobiles, and activities was now completely silent. The world felt empty. It was as if God had taken a giant gray bowl, turned it upside down, and pressed it right over us. We were trapped inside, barred from the rest of the world.

We had been among the first families to arrive at the airport, and now we were not going anywhere. I was tired and hungry. I thought about the food we had eaten last night. We had feasted, thinking we were going to leave everything behind and everything to waste. Thinking about all that food made me hungrier. Then I started to think about how little we had now, and I wondered how we were going to afford new chickens, pigs, rice, and vegetables.

"Let's go back home," Grandpa said finally.

We gathered up our things and started toward the mountain road that led to our house.

"Where is Kou?" asked Grandpa suddenly.

Nobody knew, but each of us silently wondered whether he had gotten on the airplane and left his wife and the rest of us behind. I looked at Aunt Kou. Her belly was starting to show. She looked uncomfortable as she walked along, leaning forward slightly to keep a heavy bundle balanced on her back. In her right hand she clutched another small bundle, and when she paused to shift her weight, her hand seemed to grip the bundle more tightly. Her face was expressionless as she kept her gaze straight ahead toward home. I could not tell whether she was angry, sad, or just too tired to realize that she had been abandoned.

As we reached the foot of the mountain, we heard the sound of car tires on gravel and the loud, successive honking of a horn. We turned and stared in disbelief to see a Jeep with Uncle Kou at the wheel. He told us later that he had gotten the Jeep from an American friend who had abandoned it. We climbed on, and he drove us home.

Chapter 5

All that night as I lay in bed, dogs barked continually, as if delivering messages to one another. I had a fitful sleep. Every time I woke up, I saw the faint glow of the kerosene lamp through the wide crack under the bedroom door and could hear Grandpa and Uncle Kou talking in low voices. They had been talking since dinner. I was not sure if I dreamt it, but I heard words such as "exterminate," "Miao," and "arrest." I did not know when I finally fell asleep, but the next thing I remembered was being awoken by my sister.

"Wake up, Blong," Ka-Ying hissed urgently, shaking my shoulder. "We are about to leave. We are going to Thailand now."

"Why so early?" I murmured, reluctant to wake up.

"It's already morning! You better wash up and eat before we leave, or you will be hungry later." Satisfied that I was fully awake, she hurried away to tend to other tasks.

As I made my way out of the bedroom, which my sister and I shared with my grandparents, I saw that breakfast had already been set. I hurried outside to splash water on my face and then came back in for breakfast. I didn't even dry my hands, and for the first time, my uncle did not yell at me about it. I guessed he was too tired or too busy thinking about the journey. We ate in silence. After breakfast, we all climbed into the Jeep—except for Grandpa. He came over to me, spat on his hand, and gently patted my head, which meant that he loved me and was wishing me a safe journey.

"Aren't you coming with us?" I asked.

"No. I must go to Phu Ka," he replied.

Phu Ka, my grandfather's home village, was remote, and the only way there was by foot. It took about a good day's walk to reach it. My grandfather's brothers and their families still lived there. He needed to ask if they would also be fleeing to Thailand.

I was puzzled. How was Grandpa going to catch up with us if we left by car and he by foot, and if he was going to Phu Ka first too, before meeting with us again?

"Are you going to walk to Thailand?" I asked Grandpa anxiously. He had always been there to protect me. I knew I wouldn't feel safe without him.

"I'm only going to be gone for three days. The rest of you must wait for me in Na Su. I will catch up with you there."

I stood in the Jeep and watched Grandpa walk away on the narrow path that would take him up and over the mountainside in the distance. Uncle Kou got in the Jeep and told me to sit down. He drove us down the road from our house to the valley. I turned to look at Grandpa growing smaller and smaller until I could not see him anymore.

Dust swirled around the Jeep. Grandma and Aunt Kou covered their mouths with their hands. We drove past the school, which was made up of three buildings that formed a U shape around a grassy field. Every New Year, the field was used as a place for the courtship game of ball-tossing between young men and women.

Just past the school was the morning market. Only a few days before, it had been bustling with life. Vendors were calling out their goods and haggling over prices with shoppers. The aroma of spicy coconut curry, beef noodles, freshly steamed crêpes with pork and chives, and garlicky papaya salad filled the air. Young men, offering to buy a cool drink or a bowl of tapioca dessert or simply trying to get in a few words of sweet nothings, gathered around the vending stalls that were tended by blushing young ladies.

I remembered a story my sister had told me about a young lady at the market who had been carried off by a young army captain not so long ago. The young lady was not much older than Ka-Ying. She had come with her mother to the market to sell vegetables and herbs. The army captain had seen her. After briefly speaking to her, he bought all her vegetables and herbs. She and her mother were surprised but appreciative.

The next morning, he came back with soldiers. He told the mother, "I am going to marry your daughter." He was not asking her for permission. Just letting her know. The mother looked to the left and saw soldiers. She looked to the right and saw more soldiers. She screamed for help, but besides a few words of reprimand to the captain from some ladies standing nearby, no one helped her.

She grabbed an umbrella to attack the young captain, but his soldiers stopped her. Some held her hands. One took the umbrella from her. "Auntie, please, our captain just wants to marry your daughter," the soldiers tried to reason with her. They even offered her money, which she took and threw back at them.

The brazen captain picked up the young lady and carried her over his shoulder. She pounded his back with her fists, but it was useless. The mother screamed curses at the captain.

"Mother, I will love your daughter forever. I will be faithful to her," yelled the captain as he carried the young lady away.

Afterwards, the mother cried and screamed at all the people in the market who did not try to prevent her daughter's bride-knapping. Another woman, one of the ladies who chastised the young captain earlier from a safe distance, picked up the scattered money. She held it out to the mother and said, "Don't cry. Please take the money. Your daughter will have a good life."

The mother refused to accept the money.

The woman continued, "He promised to love her."

Looking haggard and wild with tears, the mother stared at this other woman and replied, "A man who does whatever he wants without regard for others will always be selfish and inconsiderate." She cried into her hands. "My poor daughter."

That incident had been the talk of the town for days. Now the market was empty. There was not even a stray animal or an empty soda bottle rattling in the wind to remind us of the life and activity that had once existed in that place.

We turned onto the road that ran alongside the airfield. Only days before, it had been busy with military airplanes taking off and landing. Now it was as open and empty as a scorched field. We passed the new movie theater that had always been filled with people. It had been a rare treat to go see a movie there, to see the Chinese kung fu stars fighting on the big screen, sometimes leaping from branch to branch as they fought. Wang Yu was everyone's favorite Chinese hero. He had long black hair and sideburns and was an expert swordsman. Every little boy wanted to be him. But there was a new Chinese kung fu star I liked even more. His name was Bruce Lee. There was something fierce and intense about him.

We circled around the old army camp and drove up another winding mountain road. When we reached the top of the mountain, my uncle stopped to stare back down at Long Cheng for the last time. Usually, even from this distance, the sounds of the village would have reached us. But on this day, all was quiet. Everyone seemed to have vanished overnight. The emptiness felt surreal. The only things we saw were spirals of smoke here and there. Uncle Kou started to whistle a popular Laotian goodbye song. Tears glistened on Aunt Kou's and Grandma's cheeks. I silently said goodbye to Long Cheng and to my mother, who was back there, somewhere. Ka-Ying reached out for my hand and held it tightly.

Somehow, I knew I would never come back to this place again.

Chapter 6

We continued our journey toward the Thai border. We would stop and wait for my grandfather in the town of Na Su, where my uncle Lue and his family lived, and then continue on to the capital city, Vientiane. At our journey's end, we would cross the Mekong River into Thailand. How long the journey would take us and what we would find there, we did not know for certain. We rumbled along, my teeth rattling with every rut we hit, and my eyes began watering from the dust that flew up from the dirt road. As the sun rose higher in the sky, I could feel its heat on my neck.

After traveling for about an hour outside of Long Cheng, we began to see small groups of people walking along the side of the road. Some were carrying their belongings in woven bamboo baskets on their backs. Others had bundles tied to their backs with a long rope or a long strip of cloth. Older children carried small baskets or bundles in their hands. As we passed these people, I caught a glimpse of an older boy with a machete in his belt. Some of the young children rode on the shoulders of their fathers, uncles, or big brothers. People moved to the side of the narrow dirt road to make room for our Jeep and glared up at us as we passed. They probably had been walking since the night before and had not yet had anything to eat. We were some of the few people who had a car.

It was strange to see this river of people flowing to who-knows-where. They had all abandoned their homes, their chores, and their responsibilities. When we reached the top of the mountain and looked ahead at the winding road that led down to the next valley and then up another mountain, we could see that the road was swollen with more people. It seemed that here in these mountains and in this valley were all the Hmong people in the world. I suddenly thought about the emptiness of Long Cheng and wondered how it was going to be possible for the families who had stayed behind, like my mother's, to simply wake up each day and continue life as usual. The line of people stretched for miles ahead and moved slowly along like a giant snake slithering up the other side of the mountain.

Just before dawn, we arrived in Na Su, a town that was predominantly Lao. Before the war, not more than twenty Hmong families lived here, but now that the Communists had won, all the Hmong who had not been able to board airplanes in Long Cheng were walking toward the Thai border. They had decided to settle in Na Su for a few days before continuing toward Thailand. This quiet town was now crowded with a sudden influx of refugees. On the day of our arrival, it was nearly impossible to find a place to stay. We were fortunate to have family in this town.

Uncle Lue, my father's oldest brother, and his family lived here, where most of my aunt's family lived. However, we were afraid that Uncle Lue and his family might have already left for Thailand. After Uncle Kou went around and talked to several Hmong families, he found out that Uncle Lue and his family were still in Na Su. They had not left yet because Aunt Lue's family could not decide if they should go or stay. They had plenty of livestock and land. It had taken them many years to reach this level of prosperity; they did not want to give up their livelihood to start over in a new country.

Also, there was a rumor going around that the Communists were not bad at all. In fact, they wanted to reconcile and forget all the ugliness of the war. They wanted to include everyone in the rebuilding of Laos. It was this very rumor that convinced many Hmong people to stay in Na Su. Thailand seemed strange and far away, and Laos had everything that they needed, wanted, and were familiar with. If the rumors were true, then surely, the Communists would not kill the Hmong but instead allow them to continue with their lives. After all, the Communists were people too.

After driving back and forth on the main road and asking directions of people we saw, we finally located Uncle and Aunt Lue's house. It was a small Laotian-style house with a thatched roof. It stood high on four sturdy wooden stilts at the base of a hill. I could see a group of boys playing underneath the shade of the house and recognized one of them as my cousin Tong. Tong was close to my age, perhaps just a year older. He often accompanied his father to visit us. Tong and I were usually the best of friends after not seeing each other for a while, and then something would happen to make us angry with each other. After a few days, we would usually be good friends again. I think the reason we argued so much was that we were both stubborn and sensitive.

Tong's little sister Lia was nearby, squatting near a tub of water and washing some dishes. Like Ka-Ying, Lia was a slender girl with long dark hair. The two girls were fond of each other. Back when they had lived with us, Ka-Ying would comb and braid Lia's hair every morning. Whenever we had cucumbers or mangoes, Ka-Ying would cut them into slender spears for Lia just the way she liked them.

"Tong! Lia!" I called out to them from the Jeep. Uncle Kou honked the horn several times, and all the children stood to see who it was.

Lia saw us, and her face lit up. With her hands dripping wet, she broke into a run, exclaiming, "Big sister! You are here!" Tong said something to his friends and then ran toward us too. Uncle and Aunt Lue came running out of the house. To our surprise, they were followed by Uncle Jer who was supposed to be in Vientiane. Their beaming smiles made me feel welcomed and happy. Tong handed me some of his marbles and told me I could play with him and his friends. Aunt Lue gave Ka-Ying and me each a big, long hug and called us her children.

Chapter 7

My cousins helped Ka-Ying and me unpack all our things in that tiny Laotian house. I had not seen my cousins for almost a year, so I was delighted to see them even though I knew that within a few days, Tong and I were going to be arguing over petty things like we always did. But we were also going to have fun. Sometimes we would be silly and goofy, especially when we wanted to avoid doing chores.

Our arrival was still fresh, so Aunt Lue was very nice to us. As we were hot and dusty from the long journey, she took us down to the creek to bathe. I stripped to my underwear and waded in the cool, clear water. Ka-Ying wore a long, faded Laotian skirt that was pulled up to cover her body, and she bathed behind the privacy of her skirt. All the women and young girls like Ka-Ying, who had reached an age of modesty, bathed in that way. Many people were gathered there to bathe and do laundry. A few small children splashed at the water's edge while their mothers washed clothes on the rocks.

"Come here, Blong, and let me wash your hair," Aunt Lue said loudly, brandishing a cake of pink soap.

I shrunk back, feeling shy. I had long been big enough to wash myself, but I guessed she still saw me as a little boy. I reluctantly went to her and allowed her to wash my hair.

"These are my brother-in-law's orphans," she boasted to the other ladies at the creek as she scrubbed vigorously at my head. "I had to raise them up after their mother left them. This one was just a baby!" Then she pointed to Ka-Ying and continued loudly, "And that one! One time she had so many lice that I told her I might have to set her hair on fire." Aunt

Lue laughed at her own joke. "But eventually, I got rid of all the lice. It took me days. Whew!"

My poor sister. She looked mortified and turned away.

That night Aunt Lue killed a chicken for dinner. Aunt Kou and Grandma helped prepare the meal. Ka-Ying and Lia helped by rinsing herbs and vegetables. Tong and I carried firewood and started the fire in the clay stove, which looked like a clay flowerpot but with extra thick walls to support a heavy pot during cooking. The clay stove had two openings for ventilation and a larger opening for firewood.

At dinner, I did not get the drumstick, but I got the drumette, the part of the wing that looked like a small drumstick. We ate and talked and laughed. I was glad that we were all happy and eating together. It felt comforting and normal during this uncertain time in our lives.

In Long Cheng, we slept on bamboo beds with blankets used as mattresses. But Uncle and Aunt Lue did not have extra beds, so after dinner, we looked for any open space in the house to make our beds. The house was divided into three sections. One section was the kitchen and living room, and the other two were bedrooms. One bedroom belonged to Uncle and Aunt Lue. Uncle and Aunt Kou were given Tong and Lia's bedroom. Uncle Jer, Grandma, Ka-Ying, Lia, Tong, and I were to sleep in the living room.

Grandma knew we were going to be up all night talking, so right before bedtime, she grabbed a couple blankets and her pillow and went to sleep on the floor in Uncle and Aunt Lue's room. Uncle Jer, my two cousins, my sister, and I made our beds next to one another's on the floor, spreading down a blanket to lie on. Another blanket was rolled up to use as a pillow, and a third blanket was used to cover up.

"Uncle Jer, how come you did not stay in Vientiane?" Ka-Ying asked when we were all settled in for the night.

"I was on my way to Long Cheng to see what the family had decided, whether to stay put or go to Thailand. However, when I got here in Na Su, I could not find a car going to Long Cheng, which turned out to be a good thing since all of you were already on your way here," replied Uncle Jer.

"When did you get here?" Ka-Ying continued with another question.

"I got here last night," Uncle Jer answered.

Ka-Ying did not ask another question, and I was glad for that. I was eager to hear about Uncle Jer's adventures in Vientiane.

Uncle Jer was the only one of Grandpa's sons who did not become a soldier in the war. Grandma, Grandpa, and all of Uncle Jer's brothers forbade it. He was the youngest and the only one who attended school. Most children, if they attended school in Long Cheng, would drop out after several years, but Uncle Jer completed all the years of schooling that was available in Long Cheng. He excelled in all his classes. Then he was sent to Vientiane to attend a different school, maybe a university. I missed him after he moved away. He was talkative, patient, and popular. His friends often came to our house when he lived at home.

My friends and I looked up to him. I did not really understand why, but after I told them that I had an uncle who could read and write small, beautiful letters, they immediately became impressed. They treated him like he was their uncle too. We all followed him everywhere when he came home during school breaks.

We always ate special foods whenever Uncle Jer came home. Grandma said that since Uncle Jer had been living in Vientiane, he was not accustomed to Hmong food anymore. Instead of our usual meal of rice, boiled greens, and a paste of peppers, green onions, and cilantro, Uncle Jer might prefer Lao food, Grandma told us.

Uncle Jer had also eaten food from other countries. He told us about coffee and French pastries, which he sometimes had for breakfast. He had eaten Thai and Chinese food on many occasions too. He said Thai food was very similar to Lao food.

I remembered the first time he made fried rice for us. He said fried rice was a Chinese food. He minced garlic, chopped onions, and sliced chicken into tiny pieces. Then he sautéed all the ingredients in a wok. The aroma of fried meat, eggs, garlic, and onions permeated the house. I had never had eggs and meat together in one dish before. Eggs were already a valuable and special food, so people either use eggs or meat in a single dish, if they had any. Using both ingredients in one dish was being wasteful. Watching the oil sizzle and the steam rise from the wok made my mouth water.

Uncle Jer divided the fried rice into equal portions for all of us and showed us how to eat it using bamboo chopsticks that he made. When I took my first bite, the warm, perfectly seasoned rice satisfied a craving that I'd never known existed. To make my portion last longer, I ate small bites, savoring each mouthful. I wondered how I could ever go back to eating plain white rice again. Whenever he came home to visit, I eagerly asked Uncle Jer if he would make fried rice. He did not say yes often. Fried rice used up too many ingredients for one meal, he said, and Grandma would not like that.

At nightfall, we children usually begged Uncle Jer to tell us about the kung fu movies he had seen. I had already heard most of his best stories during previous visits, but it was always fun to hear them again. When he told a story, I would jump in and start telling it along with him. I also reminded him about scenes he left out—at least, I did that until someone told me to shut up. As we listened to his stories that night, one of us farted. Uncle Jer laughed out loud and pulled the blanket up over our heads. I was stuck in the middle, so I could not get out quickly enough from under the covers. We laughed and giggled and struggled to be free from the stench. Uncle Kou yelled from his room for us to be quiet and go to sleep.

I didn't know when I fell asleep. When Tong and I woke up, breakfast was almost ready. Afterwards, at the table, Tong and I asked Uncle Jer to whittle wooden airplanes for us. Uncle Jer was quite an artist. He could carve tiny airplanes, cars, and guns out of thick branches of wood. We liked airplanes the best. That day he must have whittled six airplanes, three for me and three for Tong. Before long, it was already dinnertime.

That night we did not get to hear Uncle Jer's stories. Grandma and my aunts made us go straight to bed after the dinner things were washed and put away. Uncle Jer, Uncle Kou, and Uncle Lue talked all night. I fell asleep waiting for Uncle Jer to come to bed, hoping that he would come and tell us more stories.

When morning came, I heard voices outside in the yard. I rushed down the stairs to where my uncles were loading up the Jeep. Aunt Kou was standing nearby with her arms around Grandma. Grandma was crying. I was about to run to Grandma's side, but Ka-Ying held me back.

"Mom," Uncle Kou said, placing a hand on Grandma's shoulder, "I told you already. If I stay here, the Lao people here might turn me in to the government. I also need to get through the checkpoints soon. They are becoming tighter. I can't wait for Dad."

Fear and panic were heavy on my chest. I looked at Uncle Kou and then at Uncle Jer. I wanted to cry and beg them not to leave. Uncle Kou saw the desperation on my face. He left Grandma to be comforted by Aunt Kou and Uncle Jer. He came to Ka-Ying and me.

"Blong, don't worry. You and Ka-Ying stay here with Grandma. You three wait for Grandpa. I'll be back for all of you."

"But can Uncle Jer stay then?" I asked. My voice sounded shrill. At hearing me speak his name, Uncle Jer looked up and walked to us.

Uncle Kou continued talking. "No, I need Uncle Jer to come with me. He can show the guards his papers, so they will see that he is a student in Vientiane. I'll say that I have to take him back to school. Then they will let us pass through. You understand?"

I nodded but then quickly added, "Can Ka-Ying, Grandma, and I come with you too?"

Uncle and Aunt Lue were standing nearby in the yard. From my aunt's annoyed expression, I must have sounded like a brat.

Before Uncle Kou could respond, Uncle Jer placed a hand on my arm. In a gentle voice, he said, "We can't go all at the same time. It will be harder to get through the checkpoints. And what would Grandpa think if we took you? He would never allow it, would he now?"

Still desperate to stop this from happening, I said, "Grandpa would not want this. He would not want Uncle Kou to leave us!"

I could tell from his expression that Uncle Kou was starting to lose his patience. He was eager to leave, but I didn't care. "Uncle Kou!" I insisted. "Please, won't you take my sister, Grandma, and me with you?"

By this time, it seemed all the adults were getting impatient with me. Maybe except Grandma. She was crying, so I knew she didn't want my uncles to leave either.

"No!" Uncle Kou retorted firmly. "Your aunt and Uncle Lue will take good care of you and Ka-Ying. You will stay with them. You both must be good and helpful with chores. And be patient with Grandma."

"You are delaying them," Aunt Lue said.

"We will watch over you and Ka-Ying," Uncle Lue assured me.

I continue to speak to Uncle Kou. "But—will you come back? Will you really come—back for us?" I needed to know, even though I was afraid I would not like the answer.

"I promise I will come back for you," he said, his voice softer now. I could tell he was trying to comfort me again, although he was impatient to leave. He patted my head and reminded my sister and me to be good. He gestured to Uncle Jer that they needed to leave. They patted Tong and Lia's heads in goodbye and went to the Jeep.

Uncle Kou climbed into the Jeep and sat in the driver's seat. Aunt Kou was already in the front passenger's seat. Uncle Jer climbed into the back. The three of them waved farewell and drove off. Tong, Lia, and I ran alongside, waving goodbye to them until the Jeep pulled too far ahead of us. Then we stopped and just stood staring until the Jeep disappeared behind a bend in the road.

Chapter 8

We walked back inside the house, which now seemed deathly quiet. Just yesterday, we had not been able to find enough room to lay our blankets down, and the house had been full of laughter and talking. Now the house had too many empty corners. Aunt Lue paced around, complaining about how cluttered the place was. My sister and I exchanged glances. I saw a look of alarm on her face.

"Blong, move all this stuff," she whispered urgently, grabbing our belongings from where we had left them next to the hearth. Tong and Lia came to help us. We hustled with our things and the blankets into a corner of the bedroom where Uncle and Aunt Kou had slept the night before.

At breakfast, Aunt Lue's general irritation and grievances found their target. She stared at me. "How could you ask your uncle to take you with him?" she demanded, her eyes flashing with anger. "So selfish! He could be killed because of you!" Then she turned to Ka-Ying. "And you! You probably whispered words into your brother's ears telling him to create a scene in front of Uncle Kou. You wanted to embarrass me."

"They just didn't want their uncles to leave. They did not mean to embarrass you," Grandma said without looking at Aunt Lue or us.

Aunt Lue sighed deeply as if she were making a great effort to control her anger. She stared at her two children who looked both sad and bewildered. Then in a voice that was more leveled, she said to Ka-Ying, "Well, since you and Blong will be here for a while, you two must help with chores. Also, there is a family who recently fled to Thailand and left a field of rice and vegetables. I will need both of you to help me with that farm."

"Yes, Aunt Lue," we replied.

We all ate in silence. Then as if she was still discontent, Aunt Lue resumed venting. She told us how good she was to us and how badly we had treated her in front of everybody. We listened without defending ourselves. What could we say? We were living in her house now, and we were not sure for how long or if Grandpa would ever come to get us. With her large eyes brimming with tears and her lower lip quivering, Lia looked from Ka-Ying to her mother and back to Ka-Ying again.

Uncle Lue glanced at his crying daughter and said to Aunt Lue, "Stop your complaining. We are all tired. The children are sad."

After breakfast, I quietly handed Tong his marbles, thinking for sure he would want them back, for I had made his mother angry. He held up his hand in refusal, shook his head, and gave me a sympathetic smile.

All that day, Aunt Lue's angry voice was the discordant background music that we were compelled to listen to in hushed, guilty silence. My sister was so hurt by my aunt's words that she did not eat dinner that night. I could tell that she was also very upset with me, for she said not a word to me and avoided my glances. That night, she laid out our blankets in silence.

Later when everyone was asleep, Ka-Ying nudged me.

"Blong," she whispered. "Why did you plead with Uncle Kou like that? You should not have done that! Now, Aunt Lue is really angry with us."

"I am sorry I did it. I know it was wrong to plead with him. But why is Aunt Lue so angry? What did I say to offend her so?" I asked.

"You did not want to stay with her family," Ka-Ying explained. "Now she thinks you do not love her and are ungrateful for all that she has done for us."

"But, sister, she is so mean. You know I don't—" I began. Ka-Ying quickly slapped a hand over my mouth before I could finish my sentence.

"You dummy, be quiet," Ka-Ying hissed, gesturing to the open doorway. She was probably afraid that Aunt Lue might be out there in the dark, listening.

"Are you hungry?" I asked. "You didn't eat dinner."

"Yes. Now go to sleep," she whispered.

As I lay there in the dark trying to sleep, I wondered what was taking Grandpa so long. The more I thought about it, the angrier I became with him. If only he had come with us, then we could all have left together with Uncle Kou. Suddenly, I felt panicky. What if something had happened to Grandpa? What would happen to Ka-Ying, Grandma, and me if he never made it to Na Su? Uncle and Aunt Kou were now gone, and so was Uncle Jer. Uncle Kou had said he would be back for us, but I didn't believe it. Instead, we would have to live with Uncle and Aunt Lue for the rest of our lives. They seemed to have no intention of fleeing to Thailand. We would stay here forever, trapped in Laos. I quickly said a silent prayer to God and to my father that nothing bad had happened, or ever would happen, to Grandpa.

Chapter 9

"Wake up, Blong." Ka-Ying was gently nudging my shoulder.

"What? Why?" I asked. It was still dark outside, and nobody else was stirring.

"I want to go to the well and fetch water for Aunt Lue's cooking today. Maybe she won't be so angry if I help her this morning. Come on quickly, before she wakes up! I don't want to go by myself; it's too dark."

I was tired and sleepy, but I remembered what my mother had said about protecting Ka-Ying because I was her brother. I stood up and stretched to fully awake. From the kitchen area, Ka-Ying grabbed the two aluminum buckets and the wooden pole that was used for carrying water. She told me to take the bamboo tube that we also used for carrying water. She said I should help carry water too, as long as I was going with her. We slipped out of the house as silently as we could, creeping down the stairs to the yard.

When we reached the well, Ka-Ying used the small bucket that was tied to the edge of the well to pull up the water. Then she used a gourd to scoop water into the bamboo tube. Soon the tube was filled, and she told me to hold it upright while she filled her two buckets. After the buckets were filled, she placed the pole through the handles of the buckets and squatted down to adjust the pole to rest on her right shoulder. She made sure she was centered between the two buckets so that they would stay balanced on opposite ends of the pole. Then she stood up slowly, lifting the pole and the buckets, which dangled from the pole. This was a different way of carrying water for us. In Long Cheng, we carried water in wooden containers on our backs.

We had to make several trips to the well to fetch enough water to fill the large, ceramic jar that was on the ground outside the house. When the jar was filled to the top and Ka-Ying could see her reflection in the darkness of the water, she covered the jar. We carried a bucket up the stairs and into the house to the kitchen area. Ka-Ying also decided to make rice.

We were hoping that when Aunt Lue woke up and found that we had filled the jar with water and prepared the rice, she would forgive us, but we were wrong. She was still angry and made it impossible for us to enjoy breakfast with the rest of the family. She complained as she ate. Her eyes followed our spoons and seemed to count every bite we took. The warm, fragrant rice, which always tasted best in the morning, felt lumpy going down my throat. Ka-Ying and I each had only a few bites, enough to not openly acknowledge Aunt Lue's anger with us but enough to keep her mental count low. Grandma and Uncle Lue ate in silence and tried not to let the tension make them choke on their food. My cousins, too, ate in silence, although they freely dipped their spoons into the two vegetable and meat dishes.

After the breakfast that we barely ate, Ka-Ying grabbed my hand, and we walked to the morning market. Since Na Su was a Laotian village, I was eager to see whether Na Su's morning market would be different from the morning market in Long Cheng. We walked by many vendors. Some were selling candy and rice cakes. I wished my sister would buy me a steamed spongy rice cake, but I knew if I asked, she would give me a lecture about wasting money. I didn't bother asking, but she saw that I was looking at them. After we walked up and down the narrow, crowded aisles several times, Ka-Ying finally turned to me and asked, "What would you like to eat?"

I was surprised that she was going to buy me hot food to eat. I thought we were just going to look around or maybe buy vegetables or meat for Grandma and Aunt Lue to cook later. I was also surprised that I had a choice in the selection. Usually, Ka-Ying would just tell me what we were going to eat.

"Let's eat pho," I said. Pho is a soup with thinly sliced beef and flat rice noodles. To this day, it is still my favorite food because each bowl, even if it is from the same pot, ends up having its own unique taste depending on an individual's preference of herbs, spices, and sauces. Some people like it spicy, some like it sweet, and some like it sour. The best part is when a person is finished seasoning his or her bowl, that person usually brags that his or her bowl is the best! Friends and families would banter, boast, eat, and sample one another's bowl just to come back to bragging about their own bowl.

"I knew you were going to choose pho!" Ka-Ying exclaimed, beaming at me. "Good choice."

We approached a noodle stall just as some people were leaving. We sat right down at the table facing the cook.

"Two bowls of pho," Ka-Ying said in Lao.

I smiled gleefully at her because she would usually order only one bowl for us to share. I clasped my hands and rested them on my lap to still my excitement and eagerness. Not only was I going to get my own bowl to mix and to season but also my sister was going to have a bowl all to herself. Whenever we shared, Ka-Ying would pretend that she was full and just help me put all the sauces and herbs into my bowl. After she seasoned the bowl, she would eat just two or three bites and then push the bowl over to me and watch me eat. Sometimes I remembered to offer her more bites, but other times I ate so fast that I forgot to ask her to have some more.

The cook set two steaming bowls of noodles in front of us. Floating in the broth at the top of the bowl were thin slices of beef and bits of green onions and cilantro. The aroma made my stomach growl and my mouth water. The cook moved the bottles of sauces closer to us. We shook

41

drops of fish sauce and hot sauce into our bowls and then spooned in roasted garlic and chili powder. Ka-Ying helped squeeze a lime wedge over my bowl so that I would get all the juice out of that piece of lime. She liked her noodles extra sour, so she squeezed two lime wedges into hers.

I hungrily took my first bite. The soft pho noodles were delicious and filling. The beef broth was robust, bursting with flavors, and oh-so satisfying! "Pho is the best breakfast food!" I thought. Before long, I had finished all my noodles. I lifted my bowl and drained the broth in one long, noisy gulp. When I set the bowl down again, I saw that Ka-Ying was staring at me with a bemused yet embarrassed look.

Before going back to Aunt Lue's house, Ka-Ying decided to buy us two sesame seed balls. They were golden and crispy on the outside, and sticky and chewy on the inside. The center was filled with delicious, sweet mung bean paste. I was glad that we had not eaten much for breakfast with the rest of the family. The food here was tastier. I even thought that maybe we had taught our aunt a lesson and that she was home at that moment feeling bad that we did not eat a lot of her food that morning.

We passed by a lady selling fabrics. She called out hello in Lao and beckoned us to her stall. We approached her, but Ka-Ying quickly told her that we were not looking to buy fabrics. We didn't want her to get her hopes up.

She gave a hearty laugh and said, "No one seems to be buying fabric these days."

She explained that she was Hmong and she just wanted to see if we were Hmong too, for she rarely saw Hmong people at the morning market. We told her that we had recently arrived from Long Cheng.

"Yes, many of our people are passing through on their way to Thailand," she said.

I was afraid she might ask us if we were also going to Thailand. I didn't want to tell this stranger anything, yet if she had asked, I would not have felt comfortable lying to her. Fortunately, the conversation changed because a young man, perhaps a couple of years older than Ka-Ying, approached the stall. The lady said he was her son and introduced us. We exchanged a polite hello and then told the lady that we had to leave.

I felt happy and hummed a tune as Ka-Ying and I walked back home. However, as we got closer to the house, we could hear Aunt Lue complaining loudly, almost to the point of yelling, from inside the house. Her voice was angry. It squeezed through the cracks in the bamboo walls and struck me right in the heart. I looked at my sister for support, but it appeared as though Aunt Lue's voice had struck her too. I held on to my sister's hand, and she squeezed mine to let me know that she would protect me.

"Let's go play for a while," I suggested.

"No, you go on and play. I'm going inside," said Ka-Ying.

"Why?" I asked.

"She has been like this since yesterday. The situation is not going to get any better. We either have to face her now or later." Ka-Ying and I slowly climbed the stairs and entered the house.

The moment we stepped through the doorway, Aunt Lue pointed a shaking finger in our faces and demanded, "Why did you two orphans take my money?"

"We did not steal your money," replied Ka-Ying.

"Don't lie to me! My sister saw you two eating noodles at the morning market," she shouted.

"I told you—maybe they had their own money," Uncle Lue protested.

My sister turned to Uncle Lue and pleaded, "Uncle Lue, heaven is above and down here is earth, I swear we did not take Auntie's money."

Grandma emerged from the bedroom. She probably knew she could not avoid the commotion. Uncle Lue seemed torn, as if he were deciding whether to defend us and risk a full-fledged argument with his wife or let her vent out her anger and hope that it would dissipate after a while. My sister's direct plea to him hovered in the air. He was probably afraid he might never hear the end of it from his wife if he intervened. Yet he appeared to be turning things over in his head, trying to find the right words to appease his angry wife.

Aunt Lue could see that her husband was wavering. She needed to act fast. "Don't anyone help those two lying thieves!" she shrieked at him.

Then Grandma and Uncle Lue temporarily lost their voices, and Aunt Lue thundered on like an angry goddess. She was at the height of her rant and indignation when Grandpa suddenly appeared in the doorway, scowling furiously.

"What's going on?" demanded Grandpa. "I could hear you all arguing from the other end of the village. Have you no shame?" I knew that Grandpa was referring to Aunt Lue, but he did not want to single her out.

Everybody remained silent, surprised to see Grandpa.

"Your two orphans took my money!" Aunt Lue exclaimed. Her voice was no longer a scream, but she pointed at Ka-Ying and me for added effect.

Grandpa turned to us and said, "I thought your mother had given you some spending money. Why did you still go and steal from your aunt?" He mentioned the money from our mother as a subtle hint to Aunt Lue.

"Grandpa, we did not steal," Ka-Ying protested as she moved closer to him.

Grandpa turned to Aunt Lue and asked, "How much money did you lose?"

Aunt Lue paused and looked at Uncle Lue as if shocked that Grandpa dared to question her.

"Well, I . . . I don't know; it must have been around thirty kips," Aunt Lue stammered.

"If Ka-Ying and Blong said they did not take your money, then maybe someone else took it," Grandma interjected in a low voice.

"If you are suggesting that my own children took my money, you are wrong!" Aunt Lue countered. "My children never touch my money unless I give it to them."

"Did you take your aunt's money?" Grandpa asked Ka-Ying and me. From his tone of voice, I knew that he believed us but was putting on a show of asking just to appease Aunt Lue.

"No, Grandpa," Ka-Ying said. "I used the money my mother gave us. She gave us one hundred kips. We spent twenty-five kips, and we still have seventy-five kips with us." She reached into her pocket and drew out a small wad of bills and held out the money to show Grandpa. "See?"

Uncle Lue shot Aunt Lue a stern look. She squirmed and finally howled out, "You two have money? How come you did not use it to buy food for the rest of the family? You are both selfish children!" With that, she stalked out of the room.

Grandpa slipped his backpack off and sighed wearily. He looked tired yet agitated by the scene that had greeted him. His eyes met mine, and he gestured to me.

"Blong," he said, "Come take my backpack and put it away for me."

I quickly moved to grab his backpack and carried it into the sleeping area that was designated for us. Grandpa followed me.

"Where is Uncle Kou?" he asked.

"He and Aunt Kou left yesterday with Uncle Jer," I answered.

"Jer was here?" He looked like the news added to his worries.

"Yes." I nodded

Grandpa paused for a moment. Then he asked, "Why did they leave already? I thought we were going together."

"I wanted them to wait for you, Grandpa, but Uncle Kou said they needed to make it past the checkpoints soon. He said that the Communists were making it harder to travel to Vientiane. He said they could not wait any longer. They had to leave right away."

Grandpa sighed and said, "We must follow them."

Chapter 10

The next morning, we woke up before there was light in the sky. Grandpa wanted to make sure we would be able to catch a ride to Vientiane. My uncle and aunt woke up early to see us off. Aunt Lue packed us a lunch for our journey. It was as if we had not exchanged angry words just the day before. I wish Tong and Lia were awake so that we could say goodbye to them too.

Grandpa told my uncle and aunt that he hoped they would follow us to Thailand. He said to them, "The new Communist government will never leave the Hmong people alone. They treated us no better than dogs before. Now they see us as dogs who turned on their masters when we helped the Americans." Uncle Lue promised that if things became too dangerous, he and his family would follow us to Thailand.

As Grandpa led the way, urgently telling us to hurry, Ka-Ying, Grandma, and I stumbled along behind him in the half-darkness. Eventually we reached the center of town. Vendors were already there, setting up for the morning market.

We headed for the cluster of small trucks, or songthaews, that were parked and waiting for their load of passengers. A songthaew is a pickup truck with two rows of seats along the sides of the back of the truck. The sides are fenced, and a tin roof provides some protection from the sun or the rain. The top of the roof is also used for baggage, but sometimes when there are a lot of passengers, some passengers sit on the roof and some stand on the bumper and hold on to the poles that support the roof. Usually, the driver would not leave until the songthaew is completely filled with passengers—passengers sitting on the benches, sitting on the floor of the truck, sitting on the roof, and standing on the

47

bumper holding on to the side of the truck or the poles. Grandpa said the trip to Vientiane would be long, and he wanted us to have a comfortable place to sit.

We learned that three songthaews were going to Vientiane. Two were empty, and one was half filled. Grandpa spent some time trying to decide which songthaew we should take. The half-filled one should be leaving soon, but there were no more seats left. If we rode it, we would have to stand or sit on the floor. That would be difficult for Grandma. There was no set departure time for songthaews. Whenever the driver felt that his truck was full, he would just leave. That meant that if we got on one of the ones with available seating, we might not leave until late in the day. Then, there was also the question of price. Each driver charged whatever price he wanted. Grandpa told Grandma to give him some money, and he went to haggle prices with the drivers as well as find out more about possible departure times.

After a while, Grandpa came back smiling. There was a man with him.

"We will take the middle car," Grandpa announced, pointing to a blue truck with no one in it yet.

"Is it going to leave soon?" Grandma asked. Grandma was not a patient woman when it came to riding in a car. She was always in a hurry, and she complained incessantly. Sometimes she would even tell the driver how to drive, although she had never driven before. She would check for traffic for the driver and tell him to go or stop. Her sense of direction and time was always off too, and she would tell the driver to go left when he should go right, or she would complain about why she had not reached her destination yet and that for sure, the driver was lost. Riding with Grandma was always a little embarrassing. Grandpa, on the other hand, would just sit back and tell me about the different sights and sceneries as we passed by them. Grandma also always got carsick, and it would take her two to three days to recover from a long car ride. Maybe that was why she was always in a hurry.

"I got a front seat for you," Grandpa told Grandma. He hoped that she would not get as sick if she sat in the front.

"Are they going to leave soon?" Grandma asked again. A note of panic chimed in her voice.

"As soon as the driver has enough people, then we will leave," Grandpa answered in frustration. "Get in the car before someone takes your seat."

The driver's assistant reached for Grandma's bundle, intending to stow it on the roof, but Grandma kept her grip on it and did not let it go until Grandpa signaled to her that it was all right. We made our way to the truck. Grandma and Grandpa sat in the front with the driver, and Ka-Ying and I sat behind them. Several minutes later, I could see that Grandma was growing impatient. She began prodding Grandpa to tell the driver to go. Grandpa just ignored her.

After about ten minutes, the driver returned with more passengers. Grandma, in broken Lao, begged him to get going. The driver looked at Grandma and made a face; but then, to my surprise, he climbed into the car and started the engine as Grandma had asked. The songthaew lumbered along through the town, the driver honking the horn while his assistant shouted out our destination and the names of towns along the way. The driver drove around the town a few more times. He was able to fill his truck and even found passengers who were willing to sit on the roof or stand on the bumper and hold on to the side. We left Na Su just after dawn.

Chapter 11

I must have dozed off during the trip from Na Su. The bouncy movement of the songthaew and the warm, humid air competing with an occasional cool breeze made me drowsy. All I remembered were visions of small, lonely houses along the way as I drifted in and out of sleep. Suddenly I was jolted awake by the abrupt stop of the songthaew and the sound of cars honking and bicycles bells tinkling. As I opened my eyes, the first sight I saw was Grandma hanging her head out the window like she had just finished throwing up. I looked around and saw people everywhere: people on buses, people on songthaews, people on bikes, and people walking around on foot. The sights and sounds pressed in on me, and I felt overwhelmed and confused.

I was glad Grandpa, Grandma, Ka-Ying, and I were in the songthaew and not out in the street walking around, trying to navigate our way among all those people and vehicles. After a few stop-and-go movements to avoid hitting aggressive pedestrians, the songthaew started driving at a steady, slow speed again. The bustling crowd gradually thinned out and then soon there were no more people in sight. The songthaew finally stopped when we reached a quiet, sparsely wooded area on the outskirts of town. We got out of the songthaew to stretch and take restroom breaks, which was done behind bushes or trees.

It was late in the afternoon. People started setting up tents and makeshift shelters that were made of blankets and tarp. Children began playing and running around once they realized that their parents were not going to go anywhere for a while. The older children went to gather firewood. More people arrived by songthaew. They complained loudly that a few of the Hmong leaders turned Communist and would not let Hmong people pass through the checkpoints that recently sprung up at a town called Hen-Hur. They said it was no longer just Lao Communists we had to be fearful of but that some Hmong leaders had turned into traitors and had even shot and killed other Hmong people. A look of horror momentarily crossed the faces of the listeners. Then the look of horror turned into worry, doubt, and eventually disbelief.

A lady told the talkers to stop making up stories and scaring people. Why would a Hmong person, a leader, kill another Hmong person? She sneered and dismissed the foolish talk with a quick wave of her hand. Some of the talkers gathered up their things and said that they were going back to what was left of home. As they started walking away, they declared loudly that if the country went back to the way it was, those traitors would be punished. Some of the talkers said it was late in the day so they would make camp there and go back home the next day. Others said that they would rest for the night and tomorrow search for alternative routes to bypass the checkpoints and proceed to Thailand.

We stood and watched and listened to all those people.

"I am going to speak with that man. I think I know who he is," said Grandpa, pointing to a man who had been complaining earlier. I wanted to follow Grandpa, but Ka-Ying made me stay by her.

After Grandpa was done talking to the man, Grandpa went over and talked to the driver for a long time. Eventually, Grandpa returned to where we were and said, "I have something to tell you. Tonight, we are going to a small Laotian village to spend the night. Tomorrow, we will go by boat. The driver said he has family members in that village. He thinks he can arrange with his cousin to take us around the checkpoint. He then will go through the checkpoint with his empty songthaew and pick us up on the other side to take us to Vientiane. All these things still need to be arranged, and we have to pay more money, of course."

I nodded in agreement with Grandpa. Without saying anything, Grandma looked at me with an expression that said, "You are just a kid. You don't even know what is going on. Why are you nodding your head?"

The driver went around and made the same offer to the people who arrived on the songthaew with us, and then he extended his offer to some of the other people. He found only two more families who were willing to take that chance with us. Most of the people decided to make camp and wait to see what the situation would be like the next day.

We drove for about an hour. The town was completely behind us now, and we were surrounded by lush green trees and thickets. Then the driver pulled over to the side of the road and told us we had arrived at our destination. It was not until I was outside that I saw the shimmering river nearby partially blocked by trees.

"Is all this water from the famous dam that you talked about?" I asked Grandpa. He nodded.

Back in Na Su, he told me a story about a large dam that the Japanese had built. The dam backed up the river water and formed an enormous lake that was teeming with fish. However, the Japanese had supposedly left a huge bomb somewhere in the wall of the dam. One day this bomb would explode and create a huge flood that would kill all the people in Vientiane. When Grandpa reached this part of the story, he noticed that I looked horrified, and his tone of voice quickly changed. He explained, "But it is just a rumor. Plus, if there really was a bomb, it would have gone off by now."

As I stared at the shimmering water, I was in awe of this huge body of man-controlled water. I wanted to go and see the dam up close. I hoped Grandpa was right and that the rumors were not true.

The driver led us down a small, narrow dirt path. On either side of the path were cattail-like bushes and trees. I could hear people yelling and dogs barking through those thick bushes and trees, but I did not see the village. We walked for about ten minutes and finally came out of the cattail bushes to a small, picturesque Laotian village with small bamboo huts on stilts. The red sun was about to set behind the distant mountains. I could look at the sun without hurting my eyes. The generous sun had its arms spread wide open in rays of yellow, red, orange, and other golden colors. These warm colors enveloped this small, beautiful village. The Laotian children were playing tag, and some of the men were fishing down by the dam. I instantly fell in love with this peaceful place.

Chapter 12

As we walked into the village, the children stopped playing to stare in wonder at us. A small boy started chanting, "Miao," which was what some Laotians called Hmong people. I was not sure if the word was bad, but because I had heard it spoken in harsh tones before, I associated it as derogatory. Many of the boys and girls around him began laughing at us. Their laughter encouraged him to make fun of us some more. Even when we walked past them, they kept following us and calling us Miao until the driver picked up a stick, shook it at them, and ordered them to stop teasing us. They became quiet, stared at us one last time, and then ran off.

The driver stopped and told us that since there were three families in the group, he was going to separate us in order to find enough places to accommodate all of us for the night. He took us to the home of one of his cousins. When we got there, only the cousin's wife and her two daughters were home. The two girls were about my age. After the driver explained our situation to the wife, she smiled and invited us into her home. The driver took the other two families to someplace else.

We climbed up the ladder and went inside the house. We set our bags down by the door, and Grandpa asked the Laotian lady where her husband was. She said he was down by the river fishing for dinner. I was excited not so much about eating fish but about seeing how Laotians fish. I asked Grandpa if he wanted to go see the Laotian man fish since it was not dark yet. Grandpa sat down and said that he was tired. He leaned back to rest against our bags. He crossed his legs and closed his eyes.

My sister went over to the kitchen and offered to help our hostess with dinner. Grandma sat very still next to

Grandpa. Without moving her head, she nervously scanned the room. The two Laotian girls peeled bamboo shoots but frequently stared at me and giggled. I felt uncomfortable. I did not know if they were just curious about me or were making fun of me like those Laotian children did earlier. To ignore their stares, I went to see what my sister was doing. The girls followed me and asked their mother for permission to go down to the river to wash up and see their father fish. I quickly forgot that I was uncomfortable with these girls, and I wondered if I could go with them. I asked my sister to see if she would let me go too. Their mother said yes to them, and my sister said yes to me, so I went with them to the river.

I followed the girls, and we ran, cutting through other people's yards, in our haste to reach the river. When we reached the river, there were Laotian people everywhere. I felt as if I accidentally stumbled upon a secret gathering. I had no idea there would be so many Laotian people at one place on a seemingly normal evening. I thought most people would be at home like the two girls' mother or the children who were playing near their own homes when we passed by them earlier.

As I looked around, I remember thinking that this must be how Laotians enjoy themselves at the end of a day. The women were happily doing laundry or bathing by standing in the shallow part of the river and scooping water from the river with a small bowl and pouring it over themselves as they talked and laughed loudly at the jokes they told one another. Their conversations were fast like they were competing to be heard. They talked over one another or gave a loud and quick reaction to the one who was telling a story. The men were fishing some distance away with their nets and fishing poles. The children were jumping off a cliff into the lake that was formed by the backup water of the dam. These children swam around playing tag. I wanted to join them, but I was shy and didn't know how to swim.

I just stood at the edge of the riverbank until one of the girls asked me in the universal language of hand gestures to swim with them. I went into the water, but I stayed in the shallow area. I could not even float, let alone swim. I did not want the girls to know that I could not swim, so occasionally I took a deep breath and held it as I submerged myself and swam underwater. Gradually, I became brave enough to play tag with the two girls in the shallow water.

I was having a wonderful time until I thought I heard the word "Miao" in a boy's voice. I looked around and saw the same boy who had called us names earlier. He started talking Lao to me, which I did not quite understand, but the girls responded to him on my behalf. I didn't know what the girls said to him, but it seemed like he became angrier. I wanted to know what the girls had said, but it was too late already. He jumped in the water and wanted to fight me. I was scared since I did not know how to swim, but I did not want to run either. Ready or not, I made my decision to go down fighting. I put up one fist in front of me and the other one behind my back. I stood firmly, ready to fight. The Laotian boy said something to me and gestured to the arm that was behind my back. I guessed he probably wanted to know what was behind my back. In broken Lao, I just told him it was none of his business. Neither of us threw a punch. We just moved around in a circle like we were going to fight. Then some of the kids noticed us and screamed something like "fight! fight!" in Lao.

Suddenly a loud voice rose above the commotion of these young spectators. We all turned around and saw a man carrying a huge fish on a rope in one hand and a basket in the other hand. It was the biggest fish I ever saw! Everybody quickly forgot about the fight and rushed to see the large fish. After everybody had a chance to see and touch the fish, the man said something in Lao to the two girls, and they gathered their things and motioned for me to follow them. I did not know what to do, so I just followed them. One of the girls turned around and smiled at me. The man also stopped, turned around, and introduced himself to me as the girls' father. He asked me in Lao for my name.

"My name is Blong," I responded to him in the little Lao that I knew.

"What are you doing here?" He wanted to know.

"We are going to Vientiane, but the government blocked the road, so we had to find another way to Vientiane. A songthaew driver took us to your house," I replied in broken Lao and hoped that he understood everything I said. I also hoped that he was not angry and that he would not kick us out of his house.

"A lot of Hmong go by boat if they don't have the proper paperwork," he said matter-of-factly as we continued walking home. I was surprised that he knew that many Hmong people were fleeing Laos.

"That is a huge fish," I said to him. I spread my hands open to indicate the size of the fish. He just smiled, and we walked toward his house

Chapter 13

The next day, three Laotian boatmen showed up in two long, slender boats. Each boat had a motor attached to the back. Grandma stared at the narrow boats and stared again at the huge body of water and shook her head. She refused to get in. I knew it was not just the narrowness of the boats that scared her but that she did not trust the boatmen.

When we were at Na Su, stories went around that once in a boat, some boatmen would force the Hmong refugees to hand over all their valuables, and then the boatmen would flip the boats, dumping the Hmong refugees into the water to flounder helplessly and drown. Because most of the Hmong lived in the mountains, many did not know how to swim. For that reason, no matter how much we tried to convince her, Grandma would not cooperate. She just stood there and shook her head.

I watched the other families step into the swaying narrow boats. Another Hmong woman, who looked about Grandma's age, was also terrified. She hesitated. Her son and daughter-in-law told her not to be afraid and urgently begged her to get in. With a look of pure fear and with her eyes closed, she allowed her son to guide her into the boat. She sat down and timidly looked around.

"You see? She got in. So could you." Grandpa placed a hand on Grandma's back and gently nudged her forward.

"No, I don't want to!" Grandma twisted away from him and stepped back.

"Please, Grandma," Ka-Ying and I begged. Fear and anger were rising in me.

This was the first time that I saw Grandma truly terrified, but at that moment, I did not care about her feelings. I desperately wanted to be reunited with Uncle Kou and Uncle Jer. I would rather take my chances with the Laotian boatmen than stay behind. This might be our only opportunity.

The other Hmong families and the boatmen joined us in urging Grandma. This was taking too long. It was not good to risk attracting unwanted attention. Even the elderly Hmong woman who was scared earlier joined us in cajoling Grandma. Like a stubborn child, Grandma refused. The more we encouraged her, the farther back she moved away from the water. We were all frustrated with her. I wanted to cry in sheer frustration. However, we eventually gave in to her.

The other families looked at us sympathetically as the Laotian boatmen started the motors on the boats. I was in disbelief! We were staying behind. Our only chance was speeding away. How could Grandma allow this to happen?

As we walked up the hill from the Laotian village to the dirt road on our way back to Na Su, my sister and I walked ahead. Neither of us said anything, but we knew we were not going to have another chance to go to Thailand. With tighter checkpoints and rumors of the Communist Laotian government being more brutal toward Hmong people, whom they saw as traitors for helping the Americans, our future was bleak and scary.

I was terribly angry with Grandma for being stubborn. My body felt rigid from the anger, fear, and hopelessness that seemed to flow through my veins. If only she had just gotten in the boat, maybe we would be on our way to Vientiane by now. But we had to go back to Na Su. We might never see Uncle Kou and Uncle Jer ever again.

Then another thought crept into my head. Now, we would also have to face Aunt Lue's nagging and constant criticism. Ka-Ying and I both knew that Grandma would not intervene if we were reprimanded by Aunt Lue. I was dreading the challenging times ahead.

Without speaking to each other, Ka-Ying and I both started to slow down. I guessed both of us were thinking the same things. Neither one of us wanted to walk fast now.

There was nothing to look forward to. We slowed down and let Grandma and Grandpa pass us by. Occasionally Grandpa looked back and called out to us to catch up to them. The expression on his face made me love him even more at that moment. He looked apologetic and helpless. His stare lingered on us as if to say he was sorry for failing us. He no longer seemed angry with Grandma. He seemed to have accepted the situation.

The journey back to Na Su was tiring and lonely. It made me think of the time in Long Cheng when we had to walk home from the airport. Uncle Kou had stopped by to pick us up in the Jeep he got from his American friend.

I looked behind us. The road was desolate. My eyes traced the road into the distance. I wished Uncle Kou would suddenly appear with his Jeep to pick us up and take us to Thailand. At every bend, I hoped and prayed, but every bend was as empty as the one before. All this staring and hoping and straining to see a sight that would miraculously materialize into my uncle and his Jeep made the journey back to Na Su unbearable. My heart was aching with such emptiness that it was hard to breathe.

Chapter 14

We were back in Na Su. Ka-Ying, Tong, and I were sent to tend a farm that had been abandoned by a Hmong family who either had left for Thailand or had slipped into the jungle to join the guerrilla fighters called "Cho Fa." Entire families were disappearing overnight. No one talked openly about trying to leave anymore. Plans of leaving were only whispered, and they were whispered only to a close, trusted friend or relative. A family could be tending their farm under the hot sun, pretending to be eagerly anticipating the next harvest, and then one morning, the family would be gone. If they had a relative, he or she would act surprised and declare loudly to no one in particular that he or she had no idea the family was thinking about leaving. After a few weeks, if no relative or close friend claimed the farm or other valuables that were left behind, anyone could just take it.

The farm we took over seemed like no one had taken care of it for at least a month. The weeds had grown thicker than the rice plants. My sister, Tong, and I spent every day pulling and hoeing weeds, but no matter how hard we worked, the weeds were as thick as the day before. The humidity produced nightly dews that kept the weeds alive and healthy to choke out the rice plants. Whenever Tong and I became tired of the work and the heat, we would bicker over little things, such as who was not working fast enough or who was taking too many breaks. Ka-Ying had enough of our arguments. She told Grandpa. The adults decided it was better for just Ka-Ying and me to stay at the farm. Tong complained and said he wanted to stay because he was going to be bored at home. He just wanted more breaks, that was all. He even promised to not complain so much, but he was sent home anyways. I was kind of jealous of him, and I also missed him.

The weeds were like a villainous army that could multiply to take over a field. Every day we worked, and every day we felt that our efforts were useless. I wished Tong were still there to help us. I felt bad for starting arguments with him. But gradually, ever so gradually it seemed, the farm began to look more and more like a rice field.

One late afternoon when Ka-Ying and I were on the hillside gathering firewood for the evening, we stopped and really looked at the farm for the first time. It looked pretty, blending in with the surrounding countryside into a green, scenic view that stretched far into the horizon. We had never thought the farm was going to be this picturesque. It had been a symbol of our aunt's authority and a way for us to prove our worth to her. We worked on the farm so that Aunt Lue would not complain so much about us. It was not just the grueling work that made us despise the farm, but also the loneliness of being there. We had not expected to be taken back by the sheer beauty of the place.

I can still picture the farm, especially how it looked in the early morning. The fog was puffy and thick like clouds, and those morning clouds hovered low over the rolling hills and mountainsides. As the clouds slowly evaporated, the small farm would appear on the hillside. There was a stream on the side of the hill. The stream babbled and gurgled as it flowed down the hill to join a river. During the rainy season, some of the bigger fish could be seen jumping in the stream.

At the bottom of the hill was a tiny hut. Inside, a creaky bamboo bed took up an entire half of the hut. There was also a small fire pit for cooking. The fire pit was made up of three large rocks, all about the same size, so a pot or pan could sit on the rocks over the flames underneath. Along the wall, close to the fire pit, were some firewood. Above the fire pit hung a basket. The basket was held in place by a rope that was tied to a beam in the ceiling. In the basket were a bag of salt, several bulbs of garlic, and a few ears of dried corn. The corn could be toasted in the fire pit to make popcorn. Outside the hut, right next to the door, was a metal drum that was half-filled with rainwater or water from the river. At the side of the hut was a garden that had mustard greens, hot peppers, herbs, and surprisingly, sugarcane. On the other side of the hut was a chicken coop, and it was our job too to feed and care for the chickens. Aunt Lue emphasized that we were not to butcher any of her chickens. She wanted to sell them to make some money.

In those days people did not always farm close to their home, so someone tending the farm would have to spend a night or sometimes several weeks at the farm. During our stay at that farm, after Ka-Ying and I ate our dinner, which usually consisted of rice and ginger or hot chili peppers dipped in salt, she would sometimes make popcorn for an after-dinner treat.

Using a stick or a tree branch, we swept some of the hot ashes from the fire pit and moved it around to form a little bed of hot ashes near the fire pit. We then broke off some dried kernels of corn and sprinkled them on the bed of ashes and ember that we made. As we waited for kernels to pop, my sister would tell me stories about my mother and father and how we used to have a family. I could never get tired of hearing the same old stories. I would ask her to retell familiar stories again and again until the popcorn started popping. We laughed as we tried to avoid being hit by exploding hot popcorn while, at the same time, we searched and reached for popcorn off the dusty floor. Sometimes we would draw a line between us in the dirt, and each person could eat only the ones that fell on his or her side. Of course, I got to have the ones on the line.

The sound of popcorn jumping from the fire pit, Ka-Ying's stories of the family we used to belong to, and her laughter warmed the tiny hut and kept the night out so that I was not as scared. Oh, how I miss her laugh!

Nighttime on the farm was black and heavy like a dark, wool blanket. It completely covered a person, and sometimes when I went outside to pee, I could not make out the shape of the trees and large rocks that I knew were there during the daytime, and then I would panic and wonder if my eyes were opened or closed, for everything was just black. As the darkness pressed in on me, touching the back of my neck, my face, and my arms, I thought about spirits and wondered if someone was buried close to the farm or maybe even on the farm, for nighttime creatures howled and hooted and sometimes made noises that were uncannily human.

Chapter 15

My sister and I had been at the farm for almost two weeks. We were low on rice and wondered when Grandma and Grandpa were going to bring us some more. As we bent over the land to hoe and pull weeds, we talked loudly across the row of crops to each other. There was no one around to hear us, and talking aloud kept us at a steady pace because we did not have to stop and look at each other.

On this day, we were also angry, so our voices were louder than usual. We were angry that Grandpa, Grandma, and Uncle Lue had not shown up yet to check on us and our food supply. We thought that they would have checked on us by now. It was unlike Grandpa. He usually came to the farm at least twice a week to help us. Sometimes Tong came to the farm with him too. Tong would tell me the latest news about our friends. Ka-Ying and I were still complaining and feeling sorry for ourselves when Grandpa suddenly appeared. We did not hear him approach. We looked guilty and felt embarrassed, but he did not seem to be upset by our angry, hateful talk.

"Hi, Grandpa," I said, pretending like we had not said anything bad about him or Grandma.

My sister did not look at Grandpa; she continued pulling weeds, more rapidly than before, it seemed. Finally, she looked up, her eyes flashing with anger and said, "Grandpa, we are low on rice; can you come back tomorrow and bring us some more?"

"After we are done pulling weeds, you two are going home tonight to help Grandma and Aunt Lue prepare a feast for your uncle Lue tomorrow. He has not been feeling well for the past couple weeks, you know. We are having a feast for him. After the feast, you can bring more rice back here."

He gave us a kind smile as if to let us know that he understood our anger.

At lunchtime, my sister prepared our meal of rice and ginger root with salt. As I ate, I thought about the meat I was going to eat tomorrow. I asked Grandpa, "What are Aunt and Uncle Lue going to have for the feast?"

"We are butchering a small pig and a chicken too," said Grandpa.

"Did Aunt Lue want us to bring a chicken for the feast?" I asked.

Aunt Lue had left five chickens at the farm for us to take care of because there were a lot more insects here on the farm for the chickens to eat. She was waiting for the chickens to get bigger so that they would fetch a decent price at the market.

"No, yesterday your grandma bought a small chicken from the market," answered Grandpa.

We had not eaten meat for a long time. My mouth was salivating just thinking about the food we were going to have tomorrow. I didn't care if I was going to get the drumstick or not. I just wanted to eat some meat. Maybe Grandma might even make a paste of pepper, cilantro, and green onions to go with the meat.

After lunch, we went back to hoeing and pulling weeds. The thought of going back to town made us work faster. With Grandpa's help, we were able to finish clearing the entire field earlier than we had expected.

"Grandpa, without your help, it would have taken us at least another day to finish this field," said Ka-Ying. There was no trace of anger in her voice anymore.

"Go get your things, and let's leave before it gets dark," Grandpa replied.

It took us only a few minutes because we did not have much to pack. We each had two outfits including the ones we were already wearing. I walked quickly ahead carrying Grandpa's Hmong rifle and the clothes that were wrapped in my sister's Laotian skirt. Ka-Ying was walking slightly bent forward to balance the firewood that she was carrying on her back. The firewood was in a bamboo basket, and the basket had two straps that went over her shoulders. Grandpa told Ka-Ying not to carry so much, but Ka-Ying insisted on tightly packing the basket with as much firewood as possible.

Grandpa was carrying a long, dry log on his shoulder. He had to hold on to the log while it balanced on his shoulder so that the unwieldy log would not roll off. The log was to be chopped later or tomorrow to make more firewood. As we neared the town, I could see the lights in town flickering. It was comforting to hear people hollering and laughing instead of night animals scurrying about. I was eager to catch up on the latest happenings with Tong and the few friends that I had made.

We reached the house, and with heavy sighs of relief, Ka-Ying and Grandpa set their loads by the door. Grandma was sitting on a small wooden stool at the bottom of the stairs washing dishes. She looked up at us and said, "You three are back. It was late. I was afraid you changed your minds about returning tonight."

"Is there anything to eat?" asked Grandpa.

"Since it was so late, we thought you were not coming home tonight," replied Grandma. That was her way of saying they did not save us any dinner.

"We have not had anything to eat yet," said Grandpa, sounding annoyed.

"Ka-Ying, go prepare something for the three of you to eat," ordered Grandma. "There is some dry beef above the stove. You may cut off a strip and cook it with the sour bamboo shoots from the jar."

Then as if she realized that maybe Ka-Ying might cut off a large piece, Grandma got up and led us inside the house. She went over to the stove and cut off a small piece of beef from the dry strips hanging over the stove area. The piece was not even enough to feed one person. However, I was happy that we were going to have meat for dinner, and I did not have to wait until tomorrow.

Ka-Ying lifted the lid off the wooden rice steamer to see if there was still rice left. Fortunately, there was still enough rice for us. If there had not been any left, Ka-Ying would have had to make it, and making rice in those days took a while. She then went over to the jar of pickled bamboo shoots and opened it. The foul smell rushed out of the jar to choke my sister. She had to turn away while she reached down into the jar to scoop out some bamboo shoots.

I was standing off to the side, pinching my nose so that the sour vinegar smell would not get to me. Ka-Ying ladled the pickled bamboo shoots into a bowl and carried the smelly bowl outside. She poured out the sour juice and poured water over the bamboo shoots. She rinsed the bamboo shoots several times, each time spreading her fingers over the edge of the bowl to serve as a strainer to drain out the water. When this was done, she asked me to boil water in a small pot while she sliced the small piece of beef into tiny bits. She then put the beef and bamboo shoots into the boiling water.

When she emptied the bowl of bamboo shoots into the boiling water, I thought, "Why do we have to ruin the beef soup with the smelly bamboo shoots?" But then I knew that if we did not mix the meat with the sour bamboo shoots or some other vegetable, the beef would not be enough for the three of us. The strip of dried beef was used just to flavor the soup.

Soon the food was ready. I removed the small, round rattan table from its place on a peg in the wall. The table was about ten to twelve inches high and about two and a half feet in diameter. I set the table down on the floor. My sister poured the soup into a bowl and set the bowl in the middle of the table. She scooped out rice from the rice steamer and put it in a bowl and then set the bowl next to the soup. I grabbed a small dish of pepper that was left over from dinner and three spoons. We did not use plates. I placed the three spoons around the bowl of soup.

We asked Grandma to join us, but she said she had already eaten. We sat at the table and ate. The sour bamboo soup tasted extra delicious that evening. To my surprise, there was more beef than I thought because every spoonful that I ate had some meat in it. I did not realize at the time that Grandpa and Ka-Ying pushed the beef away with their spoons and only ate the bamboo shoots and drank the broth, saving all the meat for me.

Toward the end of our meal, the door swung open, and the unpleasant smell of the sour bamboo liquid that my sister had dumped outside earlier came rushing in along with Aunt Lue. Tong and Lia were standing on either side of her. Lia's eyes lit up at the sight of us.

"What are you two doing here?" Aunt Lue demanded in a shrill voice.

"Grandpa asked us to come home to help with the feast tomorrow," answered Ka-Ying.

"How will you help? You don't know grown women's work yet. Tomorrow I want you and your brother to go back to the farm early in the morning. I don't want any thief to steal my chickens."

"Maybe . . . I can wash the dishes and pots and pans and rinse vegetables for you tomorrow," Ka-Ying suggested.

"No, Lia can do all that." She looked at her daughter.

"Ka-Ying can help me," Lia replied. "She is older and knows how to do more things."

Aunt Lue looked deeply worried. "But thieves might come and steal my chickens. Then what will we do?"

"There won't be any thieves," Tong said. "No one even goes there nowadays besides Ka-Ying and Blong."

Grandma was not happy with her daughter-in-law's complaining, but Grandma was not a confrontational person. She spoke in a low voice, "Your chickens are safe at the farm."

"Ka-Ying and Blong are just children. What could they do if thieves do come steal your chickens?" Grandpa snapped.

I could tell that Grandpa was annoyed and that he was suppressing the temptation to say more. I prayed that Grandpa would not lose his temper because knowing him, if he allowed himself to get angry now, his words would be explosive, and this fragile family harmony would be shattered.

Aunt Lue momentarily looked at Grandpa and then turned to us. "Ka-Ying and Blong may stay for the feast tomorrow, but I just know my chickens won't be at the farm anymore. Thieves will have stolen them. The money I had spent on my chickens will all go to waste!"

"We will go back early in the morning," Ka-Ying said in a quiet voice as she began clearing the dinner things. Her head was bent; she no longer had the desire or the energy to protest or beg. Lia stepped forward to help her.

"No, you and Blong will go the day after tomorrow," Grandpa said.

"It's all right, Grandpa," Ka-Ying replied. "We must return to the farm. We will leave first thing tomorrow morning."

I don't know if Aunt Lue was oblivious to Ka-Ying's sadness or just didn't care. "I sure hope my chickens have not been stolen already," she continued.

Chapter 16

Early the next morning, I woke up to my sister shaking my shoulder and whispering, "Get up, Blong. We need to return to the farm before thieves *steal* Aunt Lue's chickens!" She emphasized the word "steal."

"But it's still dark," I complained. I turned away from her without opening my eyes.

After several more failed attempts to get me out of bed, she bent down and tried to pull me up.

"Please, Blong," she said in a flat, tired voice.

I knew that she herself did not want to get up yet or go back to the farm, and I felt bad for making things difficult for her. I slowly got up even though I was tired and upset.

We went outside. She scooped water from the jar and poured some water for me to wash my face. After I was done washing, I poured the remaining water for her to wash her face. Then she went back inside the house to pack our things into the woven basket. I heard Aunt Lue telling Ka-Ying that she would pack some food from the feast later that day and have Grandpa or Uncle Lue deliver it to us. I thought bitterly that I would not touch Aunt Lue's feast food.

When Ka-Ying emerged from the house, the light of the moon shone on her face, and I could see two streaks of tears on her cheeks. She walked past me without saying anything. I had to run to catch up with her. I asked her if she was all right, but she remained silent. I knew she did not want me to hear her crying and she was probably trying to stifle her sobs, but an occasional sob escaped her throat. I tried to say words of comfort to her, but I was running out of breath from talking and trying to keep up with her at the same time.

"Ka-Ying, please wait for me," I called to her.

She just kept on walking. I jogged to catch up to her. She was talking to herself. She was saying something like, "I didn't even want the feast food. I just wanted to stay in town for a couple days."

The more Ka-Ying spoke, the more upset she became. She was now taking big strides, and even with effort, I was falling behind her again.

Soon we were approaching an abandoned military hospital. We knew that many wounded soldiers had been brought there for treatment, and many of them had died there. Some people claimed to have heard moaning and screaming from the abandoned hospital. Some even claimed to have seen glimpses of wounded ghost soldiers, bloody and with missing limbs.

"Ka-Ying, please slow down and wait for me," I begged.

She knew my fear of ghosts and my fear of the abandoned hospital. She slowed down, and I jogged to catch up to her. It seemed like the ghost stories were not on her mind that morning.

"I'm sorry I am upset," she said, "but please know that I am not angry with you. I could never be angry with you."

"I know," I replied.

"Seems like whatever I do is never good enough. I just can't please grandparents and aunt and uncle. Sometimes I think about running away to where people are not constantly finding fault with everything I do." There was no trace of anger in her voice now. I turned to look at her. She was staring straight ahead as she walked. I tried to keep up with her.

"Sometimes I wonder why you have not left, especially when I hear about young couples eloping," I said. Then I asked her, "Ka-Ying, is there someone who could take you away and marry you and then I could come live with you and him?"

If I had known what was to come later, I would not have asked her such silly questions. But I was still young and foolish enough to believe that a kind and pretty girl like Ka-Ying could be rescued in marriage by a heroic, handsome young man, and together they and I could be a family. I would be so helpful that her husband would not mind having me around. And when they have children, I would be the best uncle babysitter.

She turned to me, dropped to her knees, and pulled me into her arms. "I will never leave you. Sometimes, when I watch you playing, running around in your raggedy clothes, I wonder if I left, who would mend your clothes when they are torn. I promised Mom that I would take care of you. I will never leave you."

"Ka-Ying, you don't have to stay because of me. It makes me sad to see anyone yell at you, especially when you work hard and are always helpful. Plus, Grandma and Grandpa will take care of me."

One time when Grandpa was drunk and yelling at everyone, he said he didn't need anyone. He only needed his orphan boy because no one wanted him or me. He told Grandma that they all hated him and they all could leave. Grandma just told him to go sleep off his drunken rambling.

"I will never leave you," Ka-Ying repeated. "You are my brother. I will always take care of you."

I desperately wanted to tell her how deeply I appreciated her and that I knew her entire childhood was spent caring for me. Unable to express my gratitude, I simply said, "You are a kind sister."

She stood up, reached for my hand, and we walked to the farm.

Chapter 17

When we arrived at the farm, the eastern horizon was just starting to glow pink. The first thing I wanted to do was make sure that no one had stolen Aunt Lue's chickens. I went to the chicken coop and counted the chickens. They were all there. I went inside the hut and sat on the bamboo bed. Ka-Ying had already started a fire in the fire pit. She was bending over the rice bag, her hand feeling the contents of the bag. She let out a heavy, frustrated groan. "We rushed out of the house so quickly that I forgot to pack us some rice grains."

"What are we going to do?" I asked.

"Since we have already cleared all the weeds from our farm, we could go ask Mr. Xiong if they need help. We could work for food," suggested Ka-Ying.

It was a clever idea, but I was tired and did not want to do anything. I sat in silence and tried to think of a way to protest doing work without sounding whiny. Ka-Ying waited patiently in silence. She was too tired and frustrated to cajole me or scare me with threats of us going hungry. After some time had passed, I finally said, "I am tired! Do we really have to farm today?" To my own surprise, my voice did not come out whiny and babyish although I was close to tears. I wanted a mother or a father to pat my head and tell me to go to bed and that he or she would have breakfast on the table by the time I woke up.

"Yes!" Ka-Ying responded firmly. She emptied the last of the rice from the bag into the pot. "Go get me some peppers, green onions, and garlic, so I can make us some pepper paste."

I stood up, went outside to the small garden by the side of the hut, and gathered the things she wanted. After breakfast, my sister and I put our gardening hoes in her woven basket. She slipped her arms through the shoulder straps and let the basket rest on her back. We headed toward Mr. Xiong's farm. When we arrived, we were appalled by how overgrown the farm was. We did not see anyone, but we were certain that with all that work, Mr. Xiong would hire us to help them. We knocked on the door, but nobody answered. I pushed it open. The small, one-room house was empty. It seemed as if no one had been there for days.

"I think they left for Thailand," said Ka-Ying in a low, heavy voice.

I could not say anything at all. I knew that if I spoke, my voice was going to come out choked. The Xiongs were not related to us, but Ka-Ying and I had taken comfort in knowing that they were close by. They were friendly, and we sometimes made excuses to visit and spend several hours with them when we were lonesome. Now, their little house was empty and silent. There was an eerie, sorrowful hush over the house. I felt like Ka-Ying and I were the only two people left in the world, and my heart became heavy with that thought. I suddenly did not feel the desire or the energy to continue the drudgery of living.

"They took everything with them except this old pot," said Ka-Ying in an exhausted, defeated voice. She picked it up.

"Why are you taking that?" I questioned her.

"In a few weeks, the corn will be ready, and I am going to use it to boil corn for you." She knew I was crazy about fresh boiled corn.

I saw a red-and-blue marble on the floor and picked it up. I squeezed the marble, and the round, smoothness of it gave me something else to think about besides the emptiness of the place. When we stepped outside, I noticed that the weather had changed while we were in the house. The sky was a solid gray, and rain had started to drizzle. The mountains in the distance seemed like walls that were erected for the sole purpose of isolating us from the rest of the world.

We walked back in silence. Many things passed through my mind, such as what were we going to do about dinner that night, what was Ka-Ying thinking about, and why didn't we stay in town, despite Aunt Lue's concerns about her chickens. These thoughts floated in my mind as I followed Ka-Ying. We reached the little stream, and as usual, we looked for the shallow area to cross. As we were crossing the clear, gurgling water, I happened to look at a little pool that was formed by a bend in the stream and some large rocks that helped to trap water from the stream. I saw a flash of silver in the water. I looked closer and saw that there were two good-sized fish in the oxbow pond.

"Look! Fish!" I yelled to Ka-Ying pointing to the little rocky pond.

"Don't lie to me. The stream is not big enough for fish to travel up here." She did not bother to stop to look while she was talking to me.

"Really, Ka-Ying! There are fish down there." I rolled up my pants and stepped into the shallow, rocky pond. I began reaching for a fish. It was slippery, and I could barely touch it, let alone grabbed it. Ka-Ying saw that I was in the water, so she set the pot and her basket down and came back to the stream to look.

"Oh, there are fish down there! But you cannot catch fish like that," Ka-Ying hollered. She was smiling with excitement and eagerness now. "Let's go down the stream and find some bigger ponds. I think some bigger fish have moved up." Following the stream, we ran downhill and saw that there was a bigger oxbow pond. We stopped at the big pond and surveyed it. There were several fish in it. We stared at each other and smiled. We were going to have a good dinner tonight. Someone must be watching over us, I thought.

"We need to dig a channel so that no more water from the stream can flow into the pond," said Ka-Ying.

She paused to carefully study how the stream flowed, bent to form the oxbow pond, and then continued downstream again. "We need to dig a channel here," she said gesturing to the upper end of the oxbow pond, "and direct the water straight down to join the main stream instead of letting it curve into the pond. We can then scoop out water from the pond and catch the fish and any crab that might also be in the pond."

I began moving rocks, and she started digging. In a short time, we had a direct channel that connected the stream from the point before it curved to form the oxbow pond to where it curved back from the oxbow pond. The water went rushing down the channel to connect with the straight, rapid flow of the stream. We used mud and rocks to patch up any cracks in the low wall to minimize the flow of water into the pond.

"Start emptying the water from the pond," ordered Ka-Ying.

She took off one of her plastic sandals and handed it to me. She used the other sandal to scoop out water herself. We did this by hitting the surface of the water from a side angle so that water would splash out of the pond. She remembered the pot lying on the ground nearby, fetched it, and used it while I used the sandal.

Eventually the clear water turned muddy as the pond started to empty. I could now see a few fish flapping in the shallow, muddy water. I continued splashing water out of the pond, and I saw more fish. I was excited and wanted to stop to grab one, but my sister yelled for me to continue emptying the pond. As the water level became lower, my sister told me to splash water to one area of the riverbank instead of splashing water everywhere so that if we scooped out a fish, we would see it.

When the water reached the middle of our calves, we were elated that the size of the fish had not been an optical illusion and they were indeed adequate sizes for eating. Crabs

77

were also trying to hide underneath rocks. We stopped splashing water out and started grabbing fish. We filled the old pot with fish and crabs. Sometimes a fish would slip out to land flapping on the ground, and I would have to pick it up again. A crab almost pinched me with its claw, but I quickly grabbed its back.

Ka-Ying hollered that our channel was going to break. I looked and saw that the nice, neat walls of the channel were gone. The channel was wide and shapeless now, and water was starting to flow back into the pond. Ka-Ying and I quickly began lifting rocks and grabbing crabs that were hidden underneath or behind the rocks. Within a few moments, water came rushing into the pond again, and we quickly climbed out. Our water channel had broken, and the stream was flowing in its previous direction of curving into the oxbow pond and then curving back out and continuing downstream. I hoped that this meant more fish would find their way back to the pond so that Ka-Ying and I could come back for more fish in the future.

Although the pot was not heavy, I grabbed one handle, and Ka-Ying grabbed the other. She also carried the hoes in the woven basket on her back. We looked around the countryside, and there seemed to be a promise that we would be taken care of, that no matter how terrible things got, we would be all right. I smiled and walked quickly and easily.

We had reached the edge of our farm, when Ka-Ying said, "Let's stop for a little bit."

"Why? We are almost home," I said. But she did not answer me. She walked over to a little mound, dropped to her knees to look around like she lost something on the ground, and then she started parting the soft dirt with her hands.

"Look, mushrooms!" exclaimed Ka-Ying as she pulled dark mushrooms that looked like woodchips out of the ground. She dug around the area with her hand and pulled out more mushrooms. I went over. I did not see anything.

"How do you know there are mushrooms in the ground when you can't see them?" I asked her.

"Just look for cracks in the ground. When you see it, gently separate the dirt with your hands and you will find mushrooms," said Ka-Ying as she eagerly looked for more.

To my surprise, I easily uncovered enough mushrooms for a handful simply by digging around the cracks in the ground. I also saw bamboo shoots. This must have been a bamboo field that was slashed and burned for farming, and now the bamboo shoots were finding their way back up. Ka-Ying had also seen the bamboo shoots, and we laughed with pure excitement and joy. I felt like I was in a dream in which I had just stepped into a scattering of coins, and the more coins I gathered, the more coins I saw. We walked up and down the area scanning the ground for signs of mushrooms and bamboo shoots, and whenever they were found, we greedily gathered them up. The earth was kind and generous, and we were also having such a wonderful time that it was not long before we had enough mushrooms and bamboo shoots to last us for several days, it seemed.

On our way back to the hut, Ka-Ying said, "We are not going to go hungry now."

I looked at her and smiled contentedly. The earth had provided for us.

Chapter 18

Ka-Ying and I had so much fun catching fish and picking mushrooms and bamboo shoots that we did not realize how late it was. It was almost dark by the time we reached the hut. I supposed with the day being cloudy, it was hard to keep track of time. Ka-Ying went over to the pot of rice and scooped out the rest of the rice into a bowl.

"We have enough rice for dinner," said Ka-Ying with a touch of relief in her voice. "How would you like your fish tonight?"

"Grilled!" I replied.

"Okay, but you have to help clean the fish." Ka-Ying selected a good-sized fish and gave it to me. "You clean that one, and I will clean the rest," she said as she squatted down before a long, flat piece of wood on the ground. We used the flat wood as a cutting board.

Although I had cleaned fish a few times before, I watched Ka-Ying first to make sure I would be doing it right. She placed the fish on its side on the cutting board. She held the fish in place with one hand, and with a spoon and a rapid movement toward the head of the fish, she scraped off the scales. The movement of her hand was quick, sure, and fluid. The fish scales went flying and landing on the cutting board and the ground. A few scales even landed on me.

I picked up a piece of wood from the log pile, squatted down next to Ka-Ying, and began scraping my fish. We were quiet as we worked, determined to be finished soon so that we could start cooking the fish. When Ka-Ying was done scraping all her fish, she slit their bellies and pulled out their insides. I did not know how to do that part, so she helped clean the inside of my fish.

"You could help rinse the fish," she said. "Be sure to rinse the inside of each fish thoroughly."

I was more than glad to help. Before long we were all finished with cleaning all the fish. I took a bamboo pole and split it down almost to the other end. Then I laid two fish between the split pole and tied the pole at the split end so that the pole would squeeze the fish in place. The fire pit had been lit earlier. The flames were gently waving from side to side, casting shadows in the hut. I laid the bamboo pole at the edge of the fire pit, across two logs.

"I'm going to steam the rest of the fish. It is too bad that we don't have sticky rice to eat with them. Remember the time we ate fish with sticky rice at the Laotian family's house?" asked Ka-Ying.

"Yeah, it was delicious," I replied, remembering the savory taste of steamed fish mixed with herbs and spices and the warm, moist sticky rice that absorbed all the flavors of the fish.

"I helped her prepare that dish, you know," said Ka-Ying with a touch of pride in her voice.

"Do you remember how to make that dish?" I asked.

"Of course, but I need some spices to make it taste like how we had it. So, if you want me to make the steamed fish, you need to go get me some garlic, onion, mint, ginger, and lemongrass from the garden," enticed Ka-Ying.

"I will. But watch the fish here for me." I gestured to the two fish that I was grilling like they were a precious commodity.

I hurried out to the garden. It was dark, but I remembered where each herb was in the garden. I quickly picked and pulled some of them. When I got back inside the hut, Ka-Ying had rinsed the cutting board of fish scales and blood and was now mincing garlic.

"There you go," I told her and placed the herbs on the edge of the cutting board.

81

I quickly went to check on my fish. The smell of grilled fish, smoke, burning wood, and garlic filled the small hut, and my mouth salivated while my heart danced with eagerness. I flipped the fish and saw that they were golden and crispy with a few burnt spots, just the way grilled fish should be.

I spooned rice into two small bowls and poured water over the rice the way a person would pour milk over cereal. With my spoon, I gently pushed on the cold rice, breaking it up, and then spreading it around to create the illusion of there being more rice in the bowls. I removed the small, round rattan table from the wall and set the two bowls of rice on the table.

"I'm glad we did not eat all the rice this morning," I said to Ka-Ying.

"Yes, it would be a shame to have all this meat without rice."

Ka-Ying spread out some broad, green banana leaves on the cutting board. She placed the fish on the leaves and sprinkled salt, minced garlic, and coarsely chopped herbs on the fish. She then pulled the edges of the banana leaves over the fish to wrap them up, and gently placed the wrapped fish in the rice steamer. The pot that served as the bottom of the steamer was on the fire pit, and the water inside was already starting to hiss. Ka-Ying placed the steamer on top of the pot of water and gently moved the steamer around until it fell into place.

I pulled the bamboo pole from the fire. The fish looked perfect and ready. I untied the twig and let the two golden, crispy fish drop onto a plate on the rattan table. Ka-Ying placed our wooden stools next to the table. The table was low, so a person could sit on a low stool or even on the ground to eat at the table. As I was about to pinch some meat from the fish, Ka-Ying cautioned, "Be careful, there are lots of bones. And do not burn your fingers."

I blew on the fish a couple of times. Then I eagerly plucked pieces of the meat and popped the delicious morsels in my mouth. The fish was hot and moist with a slightly charred taste. The rice was cool and still fragrant, and it absorbed the heat of the fish without taking away its flavor. At that moment, it seemed that grilled fish and rice in water were the best combination of food in the entire world. Ka-Ying and I ate in silent satisfaction. We were enjoying our food too much to carry on a conversation.

Suddenly there was a noise at the front door. It sounded like somebody was trying to get in. We both stopped chewing and looked toward the door.

"Who's there?" called Ka-Ying.

"Grandpa!" came the reply.

Ka-Ying hurried to the door. When she reached the door, she looked at the big knife that was in her hand as if she just noticed it for the first time. I did not even see her going for the knife and was equally surprised by the knife in her hand. She set the knife down against the wall by the door and removed the long, thick pole that we put across the door to barricade it from the inside.

"What took you so long?" questioned Grandpa as he walked in carrying a woven basket on his back.

"You should not have come so late," said Ka-Ying as she helped Grandpa remove the basket from his back.

"I brought you two some rice grains. Aunt Lue and Grandma also packed you some cooked rice and leftover pork with mustard greens."

Ka-Ying set the woven basket down against the wall by the fire pit and pulled out a plastic bag of pork with mustard greens and a package of rice wrapped in banana leaves. Ka-Ying poured the pork and mustard greens into the pot and set it next to the fire pit. She checked on the steamed fish. It was not ready yet. She grabbed another low stool and placed it at the table between her and me. Grandpa sat down.

"I thought you two might be hungry," he said with a smile as he stared at our fish. He seemed impressed by us.

I took out another spoon from the basket on the wall where we kept our dishes and handed the spoon to Grandpa. Within a few minutes, Ka-Ying had the steamed fish in front of us too. She placed the small pot of pork and mustard greens on the fire pit. Grandpa unwrapped the rice that he brought and put it in the middle of the table. The pot of pork and mustard greens soup started to hiss with steam, and Ka-Ying scooped some into a bowl and placed it on the table. The steamed fish with flavorful herbs and spices, the grilled fish that were charred and crispy, and the soup that Grandpa brought were delicious and plentiful.

We were having our own feast. I was eating with the two people who loved me the most in this entire world. There was no one to cut her eyes at me and make me feel like I was eating too much. That dinner was one of the best meals of my life!

Chapter 19

The next morning Grandpa went back to town. My sister and I stayed at the farm for several more weeks. Grandpa returned to help us a couple times a week. My sister and I made a few overnight trips with him into town for supplies. During those trips back to town, I enjoyed seeing and talking with the few friends that I had made, but with each trip, I learned that there were fewer of them. Several of my friends and their families had quietly left, many disappearing overnight. Some went up the mountain Phou Bia to join the Hmong rebels who were fighting against the Communist government, and some left for Thailand.

My heart ached whenever I heard the word "Thailand" although I had no clue exactly where it was. I only knew that it was a place we must reach. Once I asked Grandpa where it was, and he said it was on the other side of the horizon.

The fear that we were going to be stuck in Laos forever was always at the edge of my mind. I tried to avoid thinking about it. The thought of never seeing Uncle Kou and Uncle Jer again scared me. Grandpa was stronger when all of his sons were with him. Although Uncle Lue was concerned about the change in government, he had made no plans to leave. The way things were now, Ka-Ying and I and even Grandma and Grandpa were helpless.

It was not just the fear of Communists that weighted heavily on us daily. Whenever Aunt Lue became angry and loud, the rest of us could never find the voice to say anything back to her, not even Uncle Lue. Although unspoken, we also knew that our lives there had no future. At any moment Communist soldiers could show up, and then what would we do? I think that was another reason why Aunt Lue was easily irritated. My aunt was strong-willed, and good or bad, right or wrong, she lived her life her way. With the Communist in power now, the life that she worked hard to create for her and her family was threatened.

I could not imagine Aunt Lue being ordered around by anyone, including a Communist soldier. I was fearful for her. Her quick temper and controlling nature made her extremely vulnerable. If she were cornered, she would fight even when it was more sensible to surrender or remain silent.

With so much uncertainty, I was glad that at least I had my sister even though our lives were empty and bleak.

Ka-Ying and I were back in town, and I had fallen into the pattern of playing with Tong and my friends in the evening after my chores. One night I decided to stay out later than usual. Tong didn't want to stay out late because he did not want to give his mother any reason to be upset. Eventually, my friends were called home by their parents for supper. Times like that made me wish the sun would not go down too quickly, so I could play with my friends longer and not think about not having parents to call me home for dinner or even to fuss at me for staying out late.

After the last of my friends left, I walked back to Uncle Lue's house. Now that the excitement of play was over, I began to feel hungry. I was wondering why Ka-Ying had not come out to look for me. She usually came out around this time to find me and yell at me for staying out so late. I hoped she saved some food for me. I was near the house now. I had to think about how I was going to walk in the house without drawing too much attention to myself. I also did a mental check to make sure all my chores had been completed, in case one of the adults yelled at me about chores.

I knew I had stayed out too late and was in trouble, so what did I do? I decided to sit at the bottom of the stairs and waited for Ka-Ying to come outside to look for me. Soon I heard the door creak open, and I turned around to see who had opened it. Although it was getting dark, I could tell that the person was Grandma.

"Where have you been?" she demanded.

"Just around the neighborhood," I mumbled.

"You know, if you always go out and play like this, when the time comes for us to leave, we might not be able to find you. Then we would have to leave you behind."

"Ka-Ying will never leave me behind," I told Grandma confidently.

"Ka-Ying already left," Grandma said without spite. She descended the stairs and sat down next to me.

"You are joking," I said, although my mind was spinning with disbelief. This must be Grandma's way of teasing me to teach me a lesson about staying out late.

"Her friend Zoua came by to tell you that Ka-Ying had left for Thailand, but Zoua could not find you, so she told us."

I strained my eyes at Grandma's face in the growing darkness. I saw that she was not teasing. She looked sad, and her shoulders drooped.

"We had no idea she was secretly talking to a young man. We do not know anything about him or his family." Grandma started sobbing now as she continued to talk. "When I last saw her today, I remember thinking that her clothes were old and torn and that she was becoming a young lady and if we ever get to Thailand, I must find a way to buy her new clothes." Grandma wiped her tears with the back of her hands, but the tears overwhelmed her. She cried into the folds of her skirt. In a broken, muffled voice, Grandma continued, "She's a girl, and she was not meant to stay with us . . . but I didn't want her to go like this. No wedding. No gifts from us. I hope her husband knows that she is not like a stray animal from the streets. She comes from a family that loves her."

Loneliness descended on me like the growing darkness. It pressed down upon me. My chest started heaving. I began crying uncontrollably. This could not be true! I thought. My sister did not leave me. She said that she wouldn't. She was my family. And now she was gone. I ran from those stairs as fast as I could. I found my way to Zoua's house, which was nearby. When I got there, Zoua was washing dishes outside. She stopped her work and stared at me while I wiped the tears from my face. Even in the darkness, I could see her kind expression.

"Is it true that Ka-Ying left for Thailand?" I asked.

"Yes, it is true. She eloped with Mrs. Vang's son," Zoua replied.

"Mrs. Vang who?" I asked.

"You know, the lady who sells fabrics at the morning market."

I was puzzled and did not know whom Zoua was talking about.

"When did she leave?" I asked.

"Around noon," said Zoua. She resumed washing the dishes, but her movements were tentative as if she was not sure if it was proper for her to be doing dishes while I was distraught and emotional.

I could see that she had a lot of dishes to wash, and it was already dark outside. I thanked her and left.

I walked slowly back home. Tears were streaming down my cheeks. I kept my head down and tried to focus on my feet and the ground in front of my every step. My mind struggled to find the reason why Ka-Ying left me. I didn't mean it when I told her several weeks ago that I would be all right if she left. Now that she was really gone, my heart ached, and I wanted to run after her. But how would I find her? Where would I search for her? I only knew a few Lao phrases.

All these questions went around and around in my head. I had no answers. She left, and I missed her. How was I ever going to stop missing her? It wasn't like I had another sister or brother or parents to comfort me and ease the emptiness.

Just then, I heard a young woman's voice calling my name from a distance. For a moment, I thought it was my sister calling for me to come home and that this whole thing was an elaborate joke, although I knew Ka-Ying would never play a cruel joke like this. I quickly wiped my tears and scanned the darkness for her. But as the voice got closer, I realized that it was not my sister's. It was Zoua's.

"Didn't you hear me?" Zoua asked, all out of breath.

"I heard you," I said quietly.

"How come you did not answer me?" asked Zoua, lowering her voice. She didn't wait for my reply. "I almost forgot. Ka-Ying asked me to give you this money."

"Thank you," I said.

Zoua asked, "Are you hungry?"

"No," I said. I did not feel hungry anymore.

"Here is some rice and hot pepper paste. We ate all the vegetables." Zoua handed me the rice and pepper paste that were wrapped in a large banana leaf. I accepted the food and thanked her again.

"The chilies are with the rice so be careful. They are very hot. See you around." She turned and walked away.

I took a few bites of the food and rewrapped it. I walked back to the house. When I got home, Aunt Lue and Grandma were sitting together, talking. They stopped to take notice of me and then resumed their conversation. Aunt Lue had a small bundle wrapped in a purple scarf on her lap. She was in the process of untying the scarf.

To my surprise, Aunt Lue's voice sounded sad. I heard her saying something like, "Poor, poor girl. No mother and no father. She wanted to begin her life."

The tone of Aunt Lue's voice sounded like she had some vague understanding of my sister's desire to grow up and begin her own life. I wondered then if I had held her back. I felt both sad and guilty at the same time. Her entire childhood was spent taking care of me. I often thought of myself as being orphaned, but she was an orphan too. And unlike me, she had the enormous responsibility of caring for a younger sibling. I was around two when our mother left. It must have been difficult to care for a two-year-old even with help from grandparents, uncles, and aunts.

"I have these embroideries and silver coins set aside for her wedding gifts," Aunt Lue continued to Grandma, "but I did not think she would be married so soon. Now, I can't even give them to her."

My tough, domineering aunt's voice was thick with emotions. It occurred to me then that these two women, quick with nagging and criticism but restrained when it came to displaying affection, were the closest my sister had of a mother-figure in her life. Although they were harsh at times, they loved her and taught her all they knew about how to be a woman.

I could not fall asleep that night. I cried and wondered where my sister was and if she was thinking of me. I thought too about whom she married and how come I did not know that she had a boyfriend. I remembered her pressing a piece of candy or rice cake into my hand after she returned from visiting a friend or running an errand. Now I wondered if the treats were given to her by her now husband, and she had saved the treats for me.

Chapter 20

It had been a month since my sister left, and I was still trying to get used to doing things without her. The first two weeks were especially difficult for me. I had not realized how much I depended on and needed her. I missed the conversations with her, I missed her ready smile, and I missed her gentle way of coaxing me into doing chores or simply to stop pouting. I even missed the trivial things that she did to annoy me, like the way she teased me or yelled at me. With my sister gone, the days and nights seemed longer.

Besides missing my sister terribly, the weather had also become gloomy and rainy. Every day was long, gray, and wet. All I wanted to do was stay in bed, cover my head with a blanket, and wait for time to pass. I could not even do that, however. I came down with a bad toothache. It hurt so much that I could not fall asleep even at night. Sometimes the pain that was radiating from my tooth spread to the entire right side of my face, and that side would throb with excruciating pain. I would press my hand against the pain or massage it, but the act provided little relief. The pain was still there to make my life miserable, and it made me miss my sister more. I missed the way she pampered me when I was not feeling well. During some of the most painful times of my toothache, I would cry silently to myself.

When the pain was unbearable, Grandpa would smoke opium and blow smoke in my face to help numb the pain. He told Grandma to make me rice porridge. He sat with me when I ate and told me funny stories. Grandpa comforted me through a week of rain and toothache. I grew even closer to him. Now, the pain of missing my sister was not as unbearable as it was when she first left.

When the rain finally stopped, and everything was green with life, Grandpa asked Tong and me to go with him and Grandma to the farm. We were going to assess the damage on the farm due to the heavy rains. The dirt path was muddy and slippery. Tong and I slipped and fell several times. Soon we were covered in mud, but we kept laughing, which annoyed Grandma. She did not think our falls were accidental. She accused us of falling down on purpose. Then she herself fell, and we helped her up.

When we finally reached the farm, I could not believe my eyes. In just several weeks, all the rice plants in the field had grown taller than me. I told Tong to follow me, and we ran into the field to search for my cucumbers. I knew exactly where they were. I had planted them by a huge log in the middle of the rice field. The last time I saw them, the cucumber vines were already climbing the log.

When we got there, we saw cucumbers lying on the ground and sticking out from the vines that were resting on the log. The large, light green cucumbers looked like arms extending from the green, moss-covered log. These were special cucumbers. They were three times the size of regular slicing cucumbers, and the inside was always fragrant with a touch of sweetness. Their seeds were small and tender. We each pinched off a cucumber at the vine, wiped off the dirt, and took a crunchy bite. It tasted cool and refreshing like water with a touch of sugar. Then the piece of cucumber in my mouth hit my aching tooth. The pain was so sharp that I almost wet my pants.

Tong burst out laughing at my initial expression. Then he looked concerned when he saw that I was grimacing in pain. "Is it your toothache?"

I told him yes. He suggested that since I could not enjoy the cucumbers, we should save them. We broke off some leaves and covered them so I could eat them when my tooth felt better. But later during lunchtime, we did not have anything to eat with the plain rice, so we went and picked my cucumbers. I had to chew my food carefully.

For the next month, my grandparents, Tong, and I went to work on the farm almost every day, but we seldom slept at the farm. We went very early before dawn and farmed all day and came back before nightfall. Sometimes I was tired of waking up early. I wished we could just sleep at the farm, but Grandpa said it was not safe to sleep at the farm anymore. He said with the Hmong "Cho Fa" guerrillas forming, the Communists were more determined to punish the Hmong.

Sometimes my uncle, aunt, and Lia came to help at the farm. My uncle and aunt frequently argued all morning over petty things, and by lunchtime, they would have a full-fledged fight. Aunt Lue would take Lia and Tong and run off to her family for several weeks to calm down, supposedly. But always before she left, she would demand that when she returned from visiting her family, she expected the farming to be completed.

From what Grandpa told me, Aunt Lue had been doing this ever since Uncle Lue married her. She and Uncle Lue would fight when there was farm work to be done, and she would run away to her family, but when the farm work was finished, she would return, saying that she only returned because her family commanded her to, as if anyone could ever command my aunt to do anything she did not want to do.

I was often perplexed as to why my gentle, soft-spoken uncle would put up with my volatile aunt, but from what Grandma told me once, Aunt Lue was a great beauty when she was young. She was the most beautiful girl in her village, and she proudly flaunted her beauty, Grandma explained. Even at a youthful age, she stared confidently back at men with her half-moon-shaped eyes and fluttered her lashes. She let her thick black hair hang shimmering down her back and refused to tie it up when it came time to cook.

Several young men courted her and were scarred by the lashes of her sharp tongue. Some of the highly respected and prominent married men wanted to marry her as a second wife, which was considered a trophy position by some people and a position of servitude by others because a second wife would have to answer to her husband and the first wife. Aunt Lue scoffed at those men and wounded them with scathing words.

Her parents were starting to fear that their arrogant, beautiful daughter was going to be a spinster. With her beauty, she could have secured a most advantageous marriage if she had learned to be demure. Instead, her parents found themselves in a constant predicament of apologizing to people whom she had offended, some of whom were powerful and well-connected men.

Then one year, at a New Year festival, Uncle Lue showed up. New Year celebrations usually lasted several days, and each village had its own. Therefore, it was common for young men to travel to other villages during New Year to court young women. Uncle Lue saw her, surrounded by multiple suitors, playing ball toss. He dared not approach her. In fact, he felt sorry for the suitors, for he saw that she could go from sweet and flirtatious to condescending and dismissive without warning. But while in the middle of a conversation with a suitor who seemed to be a favorite at the moment, she looked up and made eye contact with Uncle Lue. His face instantly burned with embarrassment. He found himself staring at the dusty ground. On that day, Aunt Lue fell in love.

Chapter 21

With Aunt Lue and my cousins away, Uncle Lue had more discretionary time, and he helped with the farming. We finished the work on the farm a couple of days earlier than expected. It was late in the afternoon on the day that we finished, and we gathered some firewood and began our trek back into town. In our eagerness to get the farming done that day, we had skipped breakfast and lunch, so all of us were famished. When we reached Uncle Lue's house, Grandma told me to start a fire in the clay stove. She went to pick vegetables and some herbs from the nearby garden.

Choosing the small dry pieces that were sure to quickly catch on fire, I gladly gathered an armload of firewood from the pile next to the house and went inside to build a fire. I took out a knife and split one of the small logs into kindling. I waved my hand over the ashes and noticed that they were still warm, so I took a stick and parted the ashes to see if I could find any charcoals that were still burning. Usually, the person who did the cooking last would cover a few pieces of charcoal to be used to start the fire for the next meal.

I dug around and found a few of the charcoals that were still burning. I placed the charcoal in the middle of the clay stove and crisscrossed the kindling pieces over them. After the kindling started to glow orange from being lit, I took the bigger pieces of wood that I had split with the knife and placed them on top of the charcoal and blew on them. The clay stove started to smoke, and the smoke stung my eyes. I continued to blow at the orange glow until it flared up into a small flame, and then I spread the logs around the flame.

When I stood up, my head started to spin, probably from the dusty ashes and the smoke. As I blinked my eyes to focus my sight, I thought I saw two ghosts standing at the corner of the room. But my eyes quickly recovered from the smoke, and what I thought were ghosts became Uncle Kou and Uncle Lue.

"Uncle Kou?" I asked, still unsure if my eyes were playing a trick on me.

"Yes," he answered and gestured with his hand for me to not speak so loudly.

I bolted across the room and wrapped my arms around him. Tears started rolling down my cheeks, and I found myself sobbing with happiness and relief.

"Don't cry, I'm here to take you to Thailand," said Uncle Kou.

"Did you see my sister?" I asked.

"Yes, I saw her, and she is doing well. When you, Grandma, and Grandpa get to Thailand, we will have her wedding," replied Uncle Kou.

"Did she miss me?" I asked.

"Do not speak so loud," Uncle Lue snapped and looked at the doorway as if he expected soldiers to be standing there.

"Of course, she missed you," Uncle Kou answered. "She told me I must take you to Thailand."

I smiled through my tears. "When did you get here?"

"I arrived this morning," continued Uncle Kou in a low, calm voice. Then, with his hands on my shoulders, he stepped back and looked at me straight in the eyes. "I don't want you to tell anybody that I'm back, understand? If any Communists knew that I was back, I would be taken away."

"Yes, I understand," I replied and nodded to underscore that I would never put him in jeopardy.

Uncle Kou gave me some money and said, "Go get yourself something to eat."

I hesitated, thinking it was better if I stayed close to home. He tousled my hair and smiled to assure me that I was not going to miss out on anything. And they would not leave without me.

96

I accepted the money and walked out the door. In the front yard, I met Grandma as she was approaching the house. She was carrying a bundle of leafy greens and herbs. She scowled at me.

"Where are you going?" she asked. A note of annoyance was in her voice. She probably thought I had not started the fire and was avoiding work.

I leaned toward her and whispered, "Uncle Kou is inside."

She looked at me like I had just lied to her. I showed her the money in my hand. Her eyes became big, and she stared at me in disbelief. Then tears welled up in her eyes. She moved quickly into the house. I did not feel hungry anymore. I followed her.

Inside the house, Uncle Kou embraced Grandma. She began crying and sobbing like I did earlier. Uncle Kou was comforting her by telling her that he would take her to Thailand to see her daughter and youngest son. All this time that we had been here, left behind, she had not shown much emotion. There were times when I was angry with her and Grandpa for not worrying that we might never leave Laos. Now as I stood there and watched her crying like a child, unloading all her worries and fears, I was overcome with emotions. The moment was sweet and touching until Grandma saw me standing there doing nothing.

"Blong, go fetch some water so I can cook dinner for your uncle," Grandma ordered.

"The jar is still full," I replied. Grandma gave me a look that told me I better find something to do. I quickly left before she thought of a task or an errand for me. Outside, I looked for Grandpa. He was by the side of the house, sitting on a low stool and smoking a huge bamboo pipe, talking to himself and smiling.

"Uncle Kou's here," I whispered to him. He did not turn around but continued to smile dreamily. Grandpa had a hearing problem. So, I leaned in closer to him and repeated that Uncle Kou was in the house.

He looked at me and asked, "What did you say?"

"Uncle Kou is in the house," I told him a little bit louder.

Grandpa leaned the bamboo pipe against the wall and went into the house. I was going to follow Grandpa back inside, but with the money Uncle Kou gave me, I decided to go to the market and buy myself a bowl of pho noodles instead. I had a feeling the adults needed to talk, and I would be in the way.

Chapter 22

Uncle Kou had been in Na Su for almost two weeks, but I hardly saw him. He was constantly on the move because he did not want anybody to know that he was in town. One night I woke up to go pee, and I saw him sitting on the edge of his bed writing.

"Uncle Kou," I said, and he startled.

"What are you doing up?" He asked, setting the note down beside him.

"I have to go pee," I told him and asked, "When are we going to Thailand?"

"Soon, but first I have to find a way for your grandparents and you to get to Vientiane."

"What are you doing this late?" I asked.

"I am working on forging a signature of one of the Communist governors," replied Uncle Kou. He gestured to the papers on the bed. "Remember, do not tell anyone about anything that we do."

"I remember," I assured him and moved closer to stare at the signatures.

Uncle Kou sat down and continued to practice writing the signature. I thought his signatures looked just like the original, but he seemed displeased with his effort and kept on practicing. After a few minutes, he said to me, "I thought you were going to go pee."

"Oh, yes," I said and walked out the door into the darkness of night. When I came back from peeing, he was gone.

The last two weeks in Na Su were the longest two weeks of my life. There was nothing to do but wait. Every day Grandma would pack and unpack her things, and each time she came across the picture of her beloved daughter

Aunt Pahoua and her family, she would cry. Grandma had always been an unaffectionate woman. Her face seemed capable of only two expressions—a scowl and a smug look of I-told-you-so. But when it came to Aunt Pahoua, her only daughter, and Uncle Jer, her youngest son, Grandma's stoicism and indifference melted away. She showed her love through food and constant worrying, and since she could not feed them or bring them food like she used to, she spent most of her time worrying about them.

When I saw her wiping away tears with the back of her hand and staring at the photo as if she was trying to pull Aunt Pahoua from it, I wanted to move closer to Grandma and comfort her, but I knew better. She was Grandma. If she saw me standing there, she would find unnecessary chores for me to do. She would tell me again to pack my clothes by rolling them into a bundle so that I could use the bundle as a pillow and yet be prepared to grab the bundle and go when the time came for us to leave. If I told her that I had already packed, she would tell me to check and repack my clothes again or tell me to go fetch more water.

Sometimes when I was bored of waiting, I would ask Grandma if I could play with my friends, but she always threatened that if I went to play, then when it was time to leave, they would leave without me. I did not want my grandparents to leave without me, so I stayed around the house and waited.

I had never been one to enjoy doing chores or working on projects or making long-range goals, but those days of waiting made life seem pointless, devoid of purpose. We ate without enjoying the taste of our food, we tended our little nearby vegetable garden knowing that we would abandon it to the weeds at any moment, and we chatted politely with neighbors without revealing too much about ourselves and inquired little of them. We were detached from everything and everyone around us. We only walked so that people would see us walk. We only went to fetch more water so that people would see us fetch water. We went through the motions of our daily lives with detachment but with the precision of automated machines. I was also fearful that we might leave before Aunt Lue returned with Tong and Lia.

There was one day when I was especially tired of the day being hot, long, and filled with nothingness that I did not refuse my friends when they came by to invite me to go swimming with them. Of course, swimming to me meant just splashing in the water because I didn't know how to swim. When I sneaked out to go, I planned to be gone for only a short while. But time flies when you are having fun, especially after weeks of being stuck in the house with nothing to do.

I was in the river splashing around with my friends when I heard a voice from a distance calling my name. With the water splashing and the noise of kids chasing each other, I was not sure where the voice was coming from. I got out of the river and looked around. I saw Uncle Kou running toward the river and calling my name. There was a bunch of kids following him calling my name too. I was surprised to see him, especially in public. I grabbed my clothes and ran toward him. When I reached him, he greeted me by hitting the side of my head with his hard knuckles and then pulling and twisting my ear. All the kids burst into laughter. My face became hot with embarrassment. Uncle Kou was tough. Whenever I did something wrong, I usually got hit, and he hit hard. I wished he would give me my beatings in private. I would rather take a more severe beating in private than a public one, even if the public one was less severe.

"Didn't Grandma tell you not to go out and play?"

"Yes," I mumbled, keeping my eyes low and away from all the jeering faces.

"Do not ever do that again, do you understand?" Uncle Kou pulled and twisted my ear harder to emphasize what he was saying. A cry escaped my throat before I could suppress it. I pressed my lips together to prevent any more cries from flying out. The laughter around me went up a notch. Uncle Kou let go of my ear and gave the back of my head a light push.

"Now go. Grandma and Grandpa are waiting for you in the songthaew up there." Uncle Kou pointed to the truck up on the bridge.

"What about my things?" I asked.

"Grandma got them. Hurry up!" Uncle Kou ordered.

I ran up the hill as fast as I could. When I got there, Grandma and Grandpa were sitting in the songthaew. I could tell by their expressions that they were angry with me. I climbed onto the back of the truck and sat quietly. The driver's assistant signaled to the driver to go. Uncle Lue was not in the truck, and Uncle Kou had disappeared from the spot where he was yelling at me earlier. I figured that I was to make this journey with only Grandma and Grandpa.

All my friends started running on the bridge, chasing and waving after the truck, yelling goodbye and good luck. I waved to them. Then it hit me that I didn't get a chance to say farewell to Uncle Lue and his family. I suddenly missed my quiet, soft-spoken uncle and my loud, complaining aunt. Although we had some tough times together, they were my family. They provided for me even when they barely had enough for their own family.

I wondered if I would see my cousins again. Tong was like a brother to me. No matter how many times we argued or fought, we were always sorry afterwards and came back to being nice to each other. I regretted that I was not always kind to him. Sometimes I provoked him when I was frustrated with other people. I suddenly felt like crying because I was ashamed for being mean to him at times. Their parents were not making plans to leave Laos. A dread came over me that I might never see them again. Uncontrollable sobs began escaping from my throat. I buried my face in my arms and cried aloud. For a moment I didn't care who was watching. I just wished I had said goodbye to Tong and Lia.

Much later when I became quiet and exhausted from crying, I started to notice things around me. We had left Na Su in the middle of the afternoon. The road was rough and bumpy after the rainy season. The jarring motion and the sudden lurches of the truck made Grandma sick. Her head was already hanging out the window. She remained in this position for almost the entire trip. Grandma looked terrible. Her hair was wild and out of place because of the wind, her eyes looked hollow and unfocused from the strain of vomiting, and her face was pale, making her wrinkles stand out more than usual. Tears also rolled down her cheeks. I did not know if the tears were the result of motion sickness or from having to travel farther from home.

We arrived in a small Laotian village at dawn. We were told that we had to stay there for the night. Grandma was carrying a couple of silver bars on her, and she was afraid that we might get robbed. She and Grandpa wanted to continue, but the driver refused to go because of the bumpy road. The driver asked my grandpa for extra money so he could find us a place to stay. Grandpa gave him the money he asked for, and he left. Later he came back and said that the money was not enough. Grandma became more afraid and thought we were going to be killed that night. She cried silently as she kneeled in front of the truck and prayed out loud to our ancestors to protect us. The driver looked at Grandma. Her hair was still wild-looking. She never bothered to smooth it back into place. He made a face of disgust as if there was something wrong with her. Then as if he could not bear the sight of Grandma a second longer, he turned and walked away without the additional money he had demanded. Later he came back and said he found us a place to stay for the night.

Chapter 23

"Get up!" shouted Grandma.

I struggled to my feet, a little dazed and confused about where I was.

"I cannot believe you. I told you to be a light sleeper, but like always it does not matter where you are, you always sleep deeply like nothing is happening. Back in Long Cheng, when the Americans or the Communists dropped bombs close to us, we forgot you several times in the house while we ran to the caves for shelter. Now you are bigger, and you can still sleep through anything. Aren't you afraid that robbers might come in the middle of the night and slit your throat? Wake up and be ready. We are about to leave."

I got up and got ready, but I hated waking up to a nagging woman who could not fall asleep because she worried too much about every little thing. I grabbed my bag and walked outside. I saw Grandpa talking to himself. I was going to ask him why he was talking to himself in the hope that he would share his thoughts with me. Sometimes after awakening from a dream that took him back to his youth, Grandpa would smile and talk to himself. When prompted, he would tell me about the dream or long-lost memories that were triggered by the dream. His stories were funny, and he seemed different in those stories. He seemed silly, carefree, and happy. He would share stories about his youth, especially how he used to court young ladies, and he would elaborate on the special ones that got away. They always sounded beautiful and charming in his stories.

But today as I walked closer to him, I realized that Grandpa was not talking to himself. He was asking our ancestors to provide us with a safe passage to Thailand and, if we came across any Communist, to soften the Communist's heart. He promised the ancestors that if we reached Thailand safely, he would sacrifice a chicken and burn some spirit money for them to repair their houses and spend on anything they wished in the spirit world. I waited for Grandpa to finish before speaking to him.

"Where is the songthaew?" I asked.

"It's not here yet. The driver went driving around the village to try to pick up more passengers for this trip. That's why he did not want to leave last night. The Laotian drivers don't want to leave until their truck is full of people." Grandpa sounded irritated or upset, I could not tell which.

"Grandpa, are you all right?" I asked.

He turned around and said, "I feel better now that I have asked your father and great-grandfather to help guide us." Grandpa knew that mentioning my dad made me feel special. I felt better knowing that my dad was going to watch over us and help us on our journey.

The songthaew came back only half full of people. Grandma began to look nervous, and I knew she did not want to board the truck. I climbed in and sat in the back. Grandma took a few deep breaths as if to calm herself before climbing aboard. She told me to scoot closer to the aisle, and she then squeezed in front of me to sit by the window. I guessed she wanted to be by the window so that she could hang her head out and vomit without disgusting the other passengers. The truck lurched forward, and pedestrians on the road quickly moved aside to let the truck pass. No one waved or shouted goodbye. The villagers went about their business without even looking up at the truck. Suddenly, I wished I had someone to wave goodbye to, a reason for waving goodbye to this remote village and these people whom I knew I would never see again.

The road was bumpy, and the trees and bushes that surrounded us made it hard to tell if the landscape was hilly or flat. Brown clouds of dust billowed behind us. Every once in a while, some of the dust floated up to my face and into my mouth and nostrils. Grandma covered her mouth and nose with her hand and tried to relax in her seat. I strained my eyes to see what was ahead and saw that there were no mountains on the horizon. However, on either side of us and to the back of us, in the far distance beyond the trees, were dark mountain ranges. They stood tall and wide like giant walls encircling us and ushering us forward. Some of the mountains were so high that they disappeared into the low-hanging morning clouds.

Eventually, the road became smoother and less wooded. The truck picked up speed. The mountains behind us disappeared to give way to rolling hills, and the few lingering, visible mountains looked thin, gray, and fragile against the sky. I tried to stay awake so that I could take in the different landscapes, but the speed of the truck and the occasional cool breezes lulled me to sleep. Before I knew it, we emerged out of the jungle into a bright sunny day. I did not realize that we had been driving through an overcast area until I suddenly found myself squinting to adjust to the blinding white sunshine.

We passed a few people walking along the streets, carrying rifles and small games that they probably caught that morning, perhaps from the jungle or from their rice fields. Soon we passed more and more people. They were carrying baskets or pushing small carts, and I knew we were close to town. I knew that farmers and country folk would often walk to town in the morning to sell or buy goods.

When we finally reached the town, I was amazed at the sheer number of people swarming about, bumping into one another. It seemed like here were all the people from the empty, desolate places we passed along the way. After all, how could those places be so empty, and this town so crowded? It just did not seem possible that these people had always been here. People were shopping, eating, hollering, walking around, and riding bicycles. I was fascinated by the bicycles and, for the next several years, often fantasized and dreamed about owning one. Sometimes in my dreams, I would pedal the bicycle so fast that I would wake up kicking off the blanket.

The truck started to slow down, and the driver's assistant announced that the checkpoint was coming up. Grandpa looked worried and told me not to say anything. The songthaew stopped in front of the gate. A soldier walked over from the guard station, which was next to the gate and talked to the driver for a little bit. Then he walked around the truck as if he was inspecting it. He stopped and asked Grandpa for some papers. Grandpa handed the papers to him. His eyes lingered on them. Grandma and I seemed to forget how to breathe. I felt like my chest was going to explode from fear. Then the soldier gave the papers back to Grandpa and asked what was in our bags. Grandpa told him that they contained clothes. He took the bags and patted the sides. Then he gave the bags back to Grandpa and asked what was wrong with Grandma. She was leaning weakly against the window. Grandpa told him she was not feeling well, and we needed to take her to the hospital in Vientiane. The soldier grimaced in disgust and handed the paper back to Grandpa and waved to have the gate opened.

We went through the gate and stopped at the markets along the street to let some of the passengers out. The food vendors on the street immediately swarmed the songthaew. They were selling sticky rice, roast chicken, fish, rice cakes, coconut desserts, and fruits. Grandpa bought two small bags of sticky rice, a curry roast chicken, three bottles of Pepsi, and two fish that came with hot chili sauce. I guessed Grandpa bought a lot of food because he was hungry like I was. I had not eaten since we left Na Su. Grandpa gave me some sticky rice and a chicken drumstick. Grandma did not want to eat, so Grandpa saved her some. The fish that Grandpa and I shared was stuffed with spices and herbs. Grandpa ate with such relish, such enjoyment, but I did not eat as much food as I thought I would.

The driver started the engine again, and dust quickly flew everywhere. The driver's assistant started calling out all the names of the towns along the way to Vientiane. Grandpa and I quickly finished our food before the dust settled on it. The day was getting late, and not many people boarded the truck. We pulled away only a little more than half full. I was thirsty and asked Grandpa if we could share a bottle of Pepsi. Grandpa took out the bottle and twisted the cap. He could not open it. Grandpa put the bottle in his mouth and tried to twist the cap with his teeth. He still could not get it to open. I did not realize that I wasn't the only one watching him. All the passengers were watching him. Their facial muscles moved like they were trying to help him take off the cap. Grandpa stopped and asked to see if any of the passengers had something with which he could take off the cap. One of the passengers pulled out a pocketknife and gave it to Grandpa. Grandpa's teeth must have hurt for several days after that, but the Pepsi tasted refreshing on that sweltering day. Pepsi was my first taste of pop, and to this day, other Hmong people of my generation and I still refer to any kind of pop as Pepsi.

Chapter 24

The road was smoother now, probably due to frequent use, and at all the military checkpoints we came across, the Communist soldiers hardly checked us. I guessed the little ritual Grandpa performed that morning for my father and our ancestors must have worked. I could see more and more houses along the side of the road as I stuck my head out the window of the songthaew. Some of those houses were beautiful and made from bricks and wood, not from bamboo, and I knew we had arrived in Vientiane. I saw what to me seemed like tall buildings at the time. They were three to five stories high. There were more people and cars than I had ever seen. Every truck was full of people. Besides people in trucks and cars, there were people in samlors, which were three-wheeled bicycles. I had heard some of my friends talk about samlors and had always wanted to ride in one.

The songthaew finally came to a stop, and we got out. It felt great to be able to stand and stretch after sitting in a metal seat for so long. I looked around in admiration and in awe of all the billboards, people, bicycles, and cars. The city was pulsating with energy. There were so much activity and noise—people yelling, cars honking, bicycle bells tinkling, and Laotian music blaring. People were sitting in the back of pick-up trucks that went up and down the street. The people on the trucks looked young, in their late teens or twenties. They were singing and waving flags in triumph and in celebration. Grandpa grabbed my hand and pulled me into a little noodle kiosk.

"What are those people in the trucks singing about?" I asked Grandpa.

"They are celebrating their victory," replied Grandpa in a lowered voice even though I was sure no one could hear us above all the noise and festivities. "I don't want you to stare wide-eyed at everything like you were just doing. Military officials will notice that you are a Hmong boy and start asking questions."

I nodded to show obedience, but I thought if they had wished to notice us, they would because Grandma looked awful from motion sickness, Grandpa carried his Hmong bag, and I had a bowl-shaped haircut, a typical haircut of a country-bumpkin Hmong boy. We definitely stood out. We even had difficulty crossing the streets. Cars were honking, and people were yelling at us. A taxicab stopped in front of us and asked us to get in. Grandpa told us to get in because he did not want the military officials who were walking in the streets to notice us. Also, Uncle Kou told Grandpa that once we reached Vientiane, we had to take a taxi to my aunt's old house. My Aunt Pahoua and her husband had already fled Laos, for her husband was a high-ranking officer in the military. They had given their house to a Laotian friend with the agreement that the friend would provide refuge to any relatives or friends who might need to pass through Vientiane to escape Communism.

After we stepped into the taxi, it slowly began moving with the traffic. The driver asked Grandpa where we were going. Grandpa did not answer him right away. Grandpa looked panicky as he stared around at this bustling city. He was probably wondering if he could trust the driver or maybe he lost the directions that Uncle Kou had written down for him. The driver drove us past some of the most beautiful statues and buildings in Vientiane while Grandpa fumbled in his bag for the directions. I stared in wide-eyed admiration at all the sights. I had never seen such beautiful, ornate structures before. Where I came from, every structure that was built had to be for practical reasons, and most of them were simple and made of wood or bamboo. I was struck by the beauty of all these magnificent places like Patuxai, which was a huge, white marble arch that was built to honor the soldiers who died fighting for Laos's independence from France.

The driver drove us around for a while, and Grandpa still could not find the directions. Grandpa asked the driver to take us to the area where Grandpa thought the house was located. When we got there, we still could not find any landmark or street that could help us locate my aunt's house. Grandma kept telling us to look for a huge tree at an intersection, but there was no huge tree at any intersection. We drove back and forth several times searching intently for a huge tree. After a while, Grandma came up with a ridiculous idea that we knock on the door of a house, any house, and ask for directions. Grandpa groaned in exasperation and called Grandma a simpleton. That was a terrible idea because those strangers could report us to the Communists.

Grandma and Grandpa started to argue. The taxi driver looked annoyed and asked us to pay him and get out of his car. Grandpa convinced him to take us to the nearest marketplace to drop us off. When we reached the marketplace, it was almost dark. The driver told Grandpa the amount for the ride. I don't remember exactly how much, but the driver and Grandpa haggled for a long time. The driver was upset with the amount Grandpa finally gave him.

After the taxi driver left, we just walked from stall to stall, hoping that we would meet other Hmong people. Maybe they could direct us to my aunt's house or help us find a place to stay for the night. Grandma and I were tired, so we sat on a bench away from all the stalls and listened to Laotian music that was blaring from the music vendor's stall. Soon Grandpa joined us and said that the vendors were getting ready to close for the night, and the Communist soldiers were going to patrol the area. Grandma became worried. She began sobbing. Grandpa told her not to worry, and we got up and walked away from the bench. We heard a voice in the distance calling, "Old man! Old man!"

We turned around and noticed a young man running toward us. We got scared, so we ran in the opposite direction. I ran so fast that I did not know when and where I had left Grandma and Grandpa behind. By the time I stopped running, I realized that I was all alone and completely lost. I was no longer tired. As I stared at the descending darkness, I wondered if this was the moment I would be forever separated from my family. The market was no longer in the distance, and there were fewer houses. I remembered what Grandpa had said about the night patrol, so I left the street.

After a little while, I came to an empty yard. I decided to sit on a large rock underneath a tree. From the citrus smell, I could tell it was an orange tree. I could hear people inside the house bantering and laughing. I even heard a television or radio program. They seemed like a beautiful family. They seemed to have everything. It made me think again of how much I wanted to belong to a family, to have a mother, father, brothers, and sisters. I was terrified and sad that I had lost Grandma and Grandpa. I decided that I would stay there for the night. If in the morning, this Laotian family found me and wanted to adopt me, I would be happy to stay with them, I told myself.

Then I saw Grandma and Grandpa walking with the young man. I panicked and thought that my grandparents had been arrested. I dropped down to lie flat on my stomach and whispered, "Grandpa." They turned around and scanned the area. They didn't see me. I was afraid that they might leave. In a slightly louder voice, I repeated, "Grandpa." He looked around and spoke aloud into the darkness that everything was fine and that I could come out. I got up and walked toward them. It turned out that the young man was the son of my aunt's Laotian friend. He had recognized my grandpa from a couple years ago when Grandpa came to visit Aunt Pahoua and her family.

"You know, we thought we lost you," said Grandpa as he placed his arm around me. "We have been searching all over for you."

I felt guilty for thinking earlier that I would allow myself to be adopted into the Laotian family.

"I know you have," I told him, "but I did what you told me to do. I just kept running until there was no danger."

Chapter 25

It was quite late when we reached the house. Mr. Jaidee, my aunt's friend, opened the door and motioned with his hand for us to quickly go inside. We had just stepped inside the house when we heard dogs barking from one of the nearby houses. Mr. Jaidee hurriedly closed the door. He did not want the neighbors to know that we were there. He directed us to the family room. This was the first time I saw a sofa. After he told us to sit down, I touched the softness of the cushions. My cousins had mentioned their sofas when they came to visit us in Long Cheng. They told me about how they stacked the cushions and jumped on them. I thought that maybe tomorrow if I felt more comfortable with Mr. Jaidee's family, I could play with those cushions.

As we sat down, I noticed that Mr. Jaidee was not as friendly as I had thought. I had confused his haste in beckoning us inside with the eager welcome of a relative who was glad to invite us into his home. Mr. Jaidee seemed kind of nervous and almost angry to see us. He told us to be very quiet and not to make any unnecessary noise. He turned to me like I was the one who would make a lot of noise. He continued to explain that some of the neighbors might report him and us to the Communist authority if they saw us.

For the next two weeks, we were not allowed to do anything. I was bored. I thought about stacking up the sofa cushions and jumping on them, but I never dared because of Mr. Jaidee. He was tense and crabby all the time. I wondered why he agreed to take over my aunt's house knowing he would have to shelter us. Maybe when he agreed to take the house, he hoped that we would never make it to Vientiane. I wished Aunt Pahoua were there to give him a piece of her mind. I met her only a few times, but I remembered her being outspoken and direct.

Aunt Pahoua was a pretty country girl who carried no trace of her country upbringing. She stood tall and erect as if she had never carried a woven basket on her back or worked in a field. She married well, and although she lived comfortably with her adoring husband in Vientiane, she never forgot her poor relatives in Long Cheng. Whenever she visited us, she came bearing gifts. She had a son my age, and whatever she bought for him while in Long Cheng, she bought the same, exact thing for me.

Even with all her comfortable, material possessions, if an elderly lady in our village gave Aunt Pahoua a modest gift of herbs, several cucumbers, or an embroidery, Aunt Pahoua would graciously accept the gift and thank the person profusely as if she had just been given a priceless jewel. She had a way of making other people feel that no matter their station in life, they were important and valued.

Mr. Jaidee was in a constant state of agitation. He fussed over every little thing. I was not even allowed to look out the window. The only time I could look out the window was when I did not hear anything going on outside. Sometimes when I heard Laotian children going to and from school or playing outside, I would run to the peek hole in the door or the little crack between the curtains and watch them. The games that they played were similar to the games that I used to play with my friends. The Laotian children seemed friendly and happy. I wanted to go outside and play with them, but I knew I couldn't.

The weather was hotter and more humid than we were used to. During the day we could not go out to bathe at the well in the Jaidees' backyard. The only time we bathed was at night when it was dark, and the neighbor's dog was not around. Sometimes I would go with Mrs. Jaidee to bathe myself. We bathed by scooping water from the water bucket and splashing ourselves, I with my underpants on, and she with her Laotian skirt covering her from the chest to the knees.

Sometimes the dog would appear and start barking. Mrs. Jaidee would yell at it while I hid behind her. The neighbor would yell from inside his house for the dog to be quiet. The cool water was so refreshing that I wondered why I ever gave my sister a difficult time when she told me to bathe.

But no matter how refreshing the water felt, by the time I stepped inside the house, the humidity was on me again. My clothes stuck to my skin, and I tossed and turned all night, unable to sleep because of the oppressive heat and humidity. I just lay in bed and waited for the night to pass.

One night when I was having trouble falling asleep as usual, I heard a noise. It was way past midnight, a time when even the dogs and other animals were fast asleep. My bedroom door opened, and I heard whispers in Lao. I pretended that I was asleep, but I did not close my eyes all the way. It was so dark that even if I had my eyes wide open, the intruders would not notice. A young lady with long hair came in and lay down next to me on the bed. My body became rigid, and I hoped I came across as being fast asleep.

She whispered something sharp and quick to the young man with her. He remained standing by the door. He turned to stare into the hallway several times. He seemed reluctant to leave the room. My eyes were starting to focus now, and I could see that the young man was Nai, Mr. Jaidee's son who found us at the market.

Nai finally left, and I was alone in the dark with this strange lady next to me. She smelled nice, not perfumed nice but fresh like you just washed yourself and shampooed your hair nice. The air seemed to thicken with more humidity than earlier. I wanted to move, adjust my position. My back was starting to ache and feel drenched. I also hoped my breathing was steady like someone who was truly asleep.

"Why does she have to share this small bed with me, especially when the night is so humid?" I wondered.

Then I heard the door open. I did not turn to see who it was. I just lay there very still. As this new person came closer, I saw through half-closed eyes that it was Nai again. He slowly climbed into the bed. The young lady did not seem to mind. But I did, thinking to myself, "Great! Now three people are sleeping in this small bed!"

They spoke in whispers, but their voices were animated and rose at times as they became exasperated with each other. Eventually, it seemed like the young lady won. I heard Nai turn to his side, away from her. She reached a hand to placate him, but he was pouting and pushed her hand away.

I remained very still, closed my eyes tight, and prayed that I would not fall off the bed, for while they were arguing, I had inched away from them. Time passed excruciatingly slow that night. My body was itchy, achy, and sweaty. I needed to readjust my position, but I had to keep still. I had to pretend I was asleep throughout all of this. I had no idea when I fell asleep, but when I awoke the next morning, both the young lady and Nai were gone. I was extremely relieved that I did not have to face the young lady in the light of day. She might not be embarrassed, but I would be.

The next night, the humidity was as stifling as usual. As I lay in bed, I wondered if the young lady and Nai would return to share my bed. If they came back again, I would not pretend to be asleep to give them privacy. I would sit up, look straight at them, and demand that they leave the room. I figured that would make them never return to my bed again. Eventually, I drifted off to sleep.

Sometime later that night or perhaps early the next morning, I heard panicked, hushed voices outside my bedroom. I stepped into the hall and saw the adults standing there, looking dazed and scared. Communist soldiers were outside the front door. They could be heard whispering, perhaps preparing to kick in the door to come in and arrest us.

The door handle rattled. Then slowly the door began to open. Mr. Jaidee pressed his hands together and prayed for divine intervention. I thought about which way I should run, and if I had enough time to grab Grandma's and Grandpa's hands.

Then the door opened. The intruders screamed. We screamed. Mr. Jaidee looked like he was going to collapse from fright. Then the Communist soldiers transformed into Nai and the girl from the night before. They had been out late and were sneaking in.

Mr. Jaidee let out a huge sigh of relief that sounded dangerously close to a sob. Only when he was completely recovered from fright and shock, then he began yelling at Nai.

Chapter 26

After that incident, Mr. Jaidee asked us to seek shelter elsewhere. Even though the house belonged to my aunt and her family, they were not there nor coming back, so the house now belonged to Mr. Jaidee. We were overstaying our welcome. Mr. Jaidee became openly rude and irritated with us. Each day I was afraid that he might turn us in himself just to finally be rid of us.

Thank goodness, Uncle Kou eventually joined us. When he showed up, Mr. Jaidee didn't even bother to be pleasant. He told Uncle Kou that we must leave his house. It was too dangerous for him and his family. His house! I could tell Uncle Kou wanted to argue with him but thought better of it. He asked Mr. Jaidee to be patient and also to give him time to find another place.

A couple of days later, Uncle Kou announced that he had found a new place for us, and we would be leaving the next day. I was thrilled because I did not feel like we could trust Mr. Jaidee now.

"It will be safer at the new place. We will be with other Hmong people," Uncle Kou explained.

The next evening, after a light dinner, we packed up our meager possessions. My things were already in my bag, which I had been using as a pillow. Soon Uncle Kou, Grandpa, and Grandma were standing in the living room with their belongings too. Mr. and Mrs. Jaidee did not bother to hide their relief that we were leaving.

"It will be better for you at the new place," Mr. Jaidee said as if he was afraid we might change our minds.

Outside, in the evening quietude, we moved quickly and furtively, sometimes hiding in the shadow of a house until we were sure that no one was around before scurrying to the shadow of another house. After some distance, we noticed that the houses were more spread out. We decided to walk on the dirt road that was made by the tire tracks of cars. We walked fast, and in my case, I had to run most of the time to keep up with the wide strides of the adults. Whenever we saw in the distance a person or people walking toward us or behind us, we would get off the road and hide behind a clump of bushes or a house until the person or people passed by. Fortunately, the road was not frequently traveled, and the people we saw appeared to be farmers who were probably too preoccupied with their own problems and worries to give us much thought. Still, we were vigilant and quickly moved off the road the moment we saw anyone in the distance.

This process of getting off the road became automatic to us. The moment Uncle Kou stopped, we all stopped, and with a curt gesture of his hand, we dispersed, darting into different hiding places. When the coast was clear, he would whistle to let us know that everything was okay, and we would pop out from behind trees, bushes, or some other place that was big enough for us to hide behind.

After a few hours, we came to an area where the houses were closer together. We would have much preferred avoiding this neighborhood, but we needed to stay close to the road. We could hear music and people laughing and talking loudly. It sounded like there was a block party going on. We cut through the backyard to get around the festivities. Some of the Laotian people saw us trudging across the mud pond that also served as a garden for water vegetations. We probably looked Laotian to them, for they yelled in Lao at us to get out. It seemed like almost every house in that area had a pond in its backyard. We pretended not to hear the people yelling at us and briskly walked on until we were on dry road again, and the sound of the party was behind us. After a while, the houses became more spread out again. Everything was quiet. For several miles we did not see a single person on the road. We began to walk freely, even daring to have an occasional conversation in low whispers. It was starting to get dark when we arrived at the new place.

The building had three levels. It stood behind several smaller houses and some tall trees. There was no one to greet us. All the doors on the first floor were closed. We climbed up the stairs and checked the second floor and then the third. Every door was closed, which indicated that all the rooms were occupied. There were families even in the hallways. We could not find a place to set down our belongings. Grandma and I went back to the first floor and sat on the stairs. Grandpa and Uncle Kou came down later and told us that they found a place. We went all the way back up to the third floor. This time without the urgency of finding a room, I took in the view from the third floor. I was thrilled to be high up. We walked all the way to the end of the balcony and stood there. I looked down, amazed at how high up I was above everything else.

"Which room are we going to stay in?" I asked.

Grandpa gestured with his hand to the area of the balcony in which we were standing and said, "This is it."

I was disappointed but looked for a place to set down my things.

"Make sure you clean the area before you put your things down," cautioned Uncle Kou.

"It is so hot and humid. I don't mind sleeping out here a bit," said Grandpa, trying to reassure Grandma that the situation was not as bad as it seemed.

I sat down on the floor and leaned back against the wall. I felt an itch on my leg and reached down to scratch. My hand touched what felt like a piece of slimy meat. I grabbed it and held it close to my face to see it better. It was a leech. I instantly dropped it and looked at my arms and body. There were leeches all over me. I began pulling them off although I was terrified and disgusted. The leeches were stubborn and sticky. When I was able to pull one off my arm, the leech would attach itself to my fingers. Grandpa pulled out his knife and scrapped them off me. One good thing about leeches is that they don't sting you like bees do. They just stick to you and slowly suck your blood.

After all the leeches were removed, Uncle Kou said, "You should go bathe." Then he laughed and added, "Make sure you check your balls really good. Oh, and don't forget to take off your clothes and wash them."

"Where is the well?" I asked.

"Down there." Uncle Kou pointed to an area away from the house.

I went down to the area where he had pointed. I saw a dirt path and followed it. I could still feel the leeches on me even though when I looked, I saw none. I arrived at the well and saw the bucket, which was tied to a rope, sitting on the edge of the stone well. I dropped the bucket into the well and swirled it around until I felt that the bucket had submerged into the water. I pulled the bucket up, but I could not find a basin to pour the water into, so I set the bucket on the edge of the well. I took off my clothes and washed myself, checking every part of my body for leeches. After I was finished washing, I realized that I had forgotten to bring dry clothes and would have to put on my wet clothes.

This year it seemed like I was more aware of my body and my appearance. I started to care about how I looked in the presence of others, even though I did not have money to buy new clothes. I knew how to take better care of my clothes now, such as patching up the torn spots and washing them frequently. Grandma liked to tell me that if I washed my clothes often, they would smell like water. I was not quite sure what smelling like water meant, but I knew if I washed them regularly, my clothes would smell better, even if I didn't have detergent to wash them with.

It was quite late in the evening. I was sure no one would come to the well this late. Still, wearing only my underpants, I hurriedly washed my clothes. I strained my ears for any sound of someone approaching. For a moment, I thought I heard footsteps. I stood up and looked around but did not see anyone, so I went back to washing my clothes. I heard a noise again, but it was only a cat. I wrung the excess water from my clothes even though my clothes needed more washing. I wanted to be finished and leave the well area. Then I heard the definite sound of someone nearby. I looked up across the well and saw a young girl who looked like she was my age. She seemed surprised and remained staring at me. Then she pretended not to have noticed me and reached for the bucket.

I quickly turned my back to her and clumsily put on my wet clothes. I had to go around the well to her side where the path was. I hoped she would move to the side, away from the path, on the pretext of looking for something, but she stayed where she was and took her time lowering the bucket into the well. Without looking at her, I walked past her and onto the dirt path. As I hurried away, I heard the faint sound of laughter from her direction. I thought how mean of her to laugh at my humiliation.

Chapter 27

For days I stayed in our corner at the edge of the balcony. I was afraid of running into the girl I saw at the well. I wondered if she told anyone about seeing me at the well. On the few occasions when I saw her downstairs in the cooking area, I tried to avoid her. Every time I looked out from the balcony and saw kids my age playing and chasing one another, I wanted to go down there to play with them. But usually out of nowhere, she would appear, running around and playing with those kids. She seemed to be everywhere I wanted to be. Sometimes I wished she would not play with boys so much and help her mother instead. I hoped that Uncle Kou would come up with a plan soon, and in a few days, I would leave for Thailand and never have to face her again.

One day as I lay on my blanket, I heard kids screaming delightedly from below. I looked over the balcony to see what was going on. I saw an older boy giving other kids a ride on his bicycle. I had never been on a bicycle before and wanted to go down to see if I could get a ride too. To my annoyance, I found myself automatically scanning around to see if the girl was nearby. I did not see her, which was surprising, especially because the kids below seemed to be having a fun time. Perhaps she and her family had already left for Thailand, or she was busy helping her mother today, I thought as I eagerly ran down the stairs.

When I reached the ground level, the line for the bike ride had grown longer than it was when I was watching from the balcony. There seemed to be more kids today than on the other days. I did not realize that there were that many kids living in the complex. The line seemed not to be moving at all, or maybe I was just afraid that the girl might suddenly show up. As I waited for my turn, I kept a lookout for the girl. Eventually, there was only one kid ahead of me, and then it would be my turn.

The older boy with the bike stopped in front of me and said, "You must be new here. I have not seen you before. My name is Vameng Thao. What's yours?"

"Blong Yang," I replied.

"In a little bit it will be your turn," said Vameng.

The kid in front of me held on to Vameng's shoulders, climbed onto the flat axle pegs that protruded from either side of the back wheel, and sat as far back as possible on the long seat. Vameng took the kid to the end of the corner and made a nice, wide U-turn to bring the kid back to stop in front of me. The kid was smiling, his eyes gleaming with joy. I was eager and excited because it was finally my turn. I climbed on the back seat, and Vameng asked if I was ready like he had asked all the kids before he began pedaling. I was just about to answer him when a voice called out his name.

"Vameng! Dad needs to see you now!" said the girl as she jogged toward us.

"Alright. Let me give Blong a ride first," answered Vameng.

"I can do it," said the girl.

I suddenly wanted to get off the bike, but I could not manage to speak up. Vameng looked at her for a moment and then said, "Here." He sounded reluctant to hand over the bike. She smiled and grabbed the handles anyway. Even though my toes were touching the ground, I almost fell off the bike as it tilted in the exchange.

"Blong is new here," Vameng told her.

"I know. We met at the well," she replied casually.

I was embarrassed and was about to get off when she quickly climbed on and began pedaling away. She did not even ask to see if I was ready. Because I was trying to get off when she began pedaling, I was not centered. The bike wobbled. It was also too large for her. She had to remain standing to pedal it.

"Hold on to me!" she yelled as we picked up speed.

I grabbed her arms.

"No! Don't grab my arms. I cannot turn," she yelled.

The moment I let go of her arms, I started to fall backward. In a panic, I instantly threw my arms around her and clutched at her front. It took less than a second for my mind to register what I had done. I had made a huge, terrible mistake!

She yelled, "Take your hands off!"

I instantly pulled my arms away, too dumbstruck and embarrassed to think of holding on to anything else. My whole body shifted to one side, pulling the bike along with me. She lost control, and we both fell. I reached out a hand to break my fall, and my hand smeared hard against gravel and dirt just seconds before the girl, the bike, and I landed hard on my arm and the side of my face.

She sprang up and darted off in the direction of her house as all the other kids ran to me. I wondered if she was hurt or just angry. By the time I got to my feet, all the kids had pulled the bike upright again. Each kid was reaching a hand out to support the bike and to help push it back to the starting point. They all examined the bike closely, squatting down for a closer inspection and turning it from side to side to make sure that it was okay. No one paid attention to me.

I walked slowly back to the complex. Pain was starting to radiate from my hand, arm, and face. I knew that if there were visible scars, Grandpa was going to yell at me for being careless. Vameng emerged from a one-level house near the complex, the very house that the girl ran into. He took the bike from the other kids and said that was enough for the day.

As I was about to climb up the stairs, the girl came out of the one-level house and ran over to me.

"Are you badly hurt?" she asked, handing me a handkerchief.

"I'm fine," I replied. I accepted the handkerchief and noticed it was damp. I wondered why she gave me a damp handkerchief.

As if she read my mind, she pointed to the right side of my face and said, "You are bleeding."

I wiped the blood from my face and stared at the red spot on the handkerchief. "Thank you," I said, feeling kind of bad for ruining her handkerchief.

She nodded and smiled. Her smile was beautiful. For half a second, her smile was tentative like she was not sure if she should smile at me, and then the corners of her lips pulled back and stayed in an expression of gentleness and sympathy. Her dark eyes softened with what seemed to be compassion, patience, and understanding. I could not believe this was the same girl who laughed at my humiliation at the well. Suddenly I did not want to give the bloody handkerchief back to her.

"Let me wash off the blood first before I give it back to you," I offered.

"You don't have to. I can wash it myself," she said.

"I was going to wash my clothes tomorrow anyway," I told her.

"Me too. Maybe I will see you at the well," she said.

My face felt hot at the thought of meeting her at the well again. "Maybe," I replied and turned to walk up the stairs.

"Blong!" she called.

I turned around.

"My name is Mayna."

"That's a nice name," I told her.

"You are just saying that," she said and broke into her pretty smile again. This time her smile was sure and confident, and her eyes sparkled with laughter. She continued, "How come you don't smile?"

"There's nothing to smile at," I answered. Then I realized I probably sounded grumpy, so I quickly added, "I have crooked teeth. If you saw them, you would make fun of me." I found myself suddenly trying to talk without showing my teeth.

"I think you have a cute smile," Mayna concluded.

Before I knew it, I smiled at her, but without showing my teeth.

"It is good to see you smile," said Mayna. "I overheard your grandma telling the other ladies that you are an orphan. Is that true?"

"Yes, it is true," I replied. We looked at each other for a few minutes and then said goodbye. When I reached the balcony, I looked down, but she was gone.

Chapter 28

It was almost noon. I had been waiting impatiently all morning for Mayna to emerge from her house. Every few minutes I found myself looking over the balcony at the ground below, in the direction of her house or in the direction of the well. I wondered why she had not come out. Just yesterday when I did not want to see her, she was everywhere. Finally, I gave up and decided to go by myself down to the well to wash her handkerchief and my clothes.

I was at the well not for long when Mayna showed up. She seemed upset and pretended not to notice me. I was upset too, for I had been waiting for her all morning. We washed our clothes in silence. I secretly hoped she would start a conversation or at least vent and tell me what was bothering her. I stole quick, furtive glances at her. She looked angry. She moved around rapidly and washed her clothes with such vehemence that I was afraid she might be finished before we both recovered from our anger to talk to each other. After a while, I gave in and asked her why she was upset.

"Oh, you finally noticed me!" she responded.

"I noticed you earlier, but you were angry. I didn't want to bother you."

"Yesterday, you told me you were going to wash your clothes today. How come you came so late? You are not going to have enough time to dry your clothes now." She sounded like she was reprimanding me. Or perhaps she was disappointed in me.

"Were you waiting for me?" I asked, being careful to hide the tone of curiosity in my voice.

She looked at me like I was crazy and did not answer. Then she began pulling water up from the well. She seemed to have difficulty. I went over to help her.

"You should not fetch such a full bucket," I told her. "It's too heavy to pull up."

"You think I cannot pull up a full bucket by myself?" Mayna snorted defensively.

"I did not say that. I'm just saying that it is too heavy to pull a full bucket of water. What is the matter? Why are you mad at me?" I was starting to feel irritated by her bad mood. What happened to the nice girl yesterday who offered me a handkerchief?

After she emptied the bucket of water into a larger metal bucket, she straightened up and turned to me. I did not realize that I was standing close to her until then. She was about my height, and I found myself staring into her eyes, which were a shade of brown so dark that they were almost black. Her long lashes did not flutter at all as she boldly stared back at me. I realized then that she looked more Lao than Hmong. She had a darker complexion than most other Hmong girls. Her cheekbones were prominent, and her nose turned slightly upward at the tip, making her seem arrogant. Her lips were full and slightly parted as she waited for me to back down from this stare. She looked prettier today than yesterday. We stood still for a few minutes not knowing what to do. My mouth was agape. I felt the need to swallow. I finally gave in to the urge to swallow and broke the magic of that moment by looking away. She turned her attention back to filling her bucket with water. She talked as she worked.

"I was not mad at you." Her voice was softer and more pleasant now, no longer harsh and accusatory.

"You seemed so cold earlier that I thought you were angry with me," I said.

"I was mad at you because you told me you were going to wash your clothes this morning, but it took you forever to come out." She emphasized the word forever.

"I am sorry. I had things I needed to do for my grandparents." I did not want to explain to her that I had spent the entire morning watching from the balcony for her to come out first.

She looked at me and smiled. I was glad we were no longer angry with each other. A thought crossed my mind that every moment spent with her should not be wasted on being petty and angry, even if I had to swallow my pride and let her win.

"You may use some of my detergent," she offered.

I was washing my clothes with just plain water.

"Thank you. Grandma and Grandpa have not gone to buy any yet," I lied. The truth was Grandma didn't want to spend money on what she considered to be unnecessary things nowadays.

"I understand," she said as she picked up her full bucket by the handle. She looked like she was straining. I rose to help her, but she held her hand up in refusal. I felt bad for not helping, but I had a feeling my good intentions could lead to another argument. She had to take tiny steps to prevent the water inside her rather full bucket from sloshing. Her tiny steps made the water slosh back and forth, but it did not splash out. I had never thought a girl carrying water was anything beautiful to watch, but there was something strong yet graceful about her movement.

"I will be right back. My mother is waiting for water," she called over her shoulder as she walked away.

Before long, she was back. She handed me a small, colorful carton of detergent.

I put the carton to my nose and breathed in its fragrance. It smelled clean and fresh with a touch of perfume. Oh, how I wished I could afford soap so that my clothes could always smell this good, I thought. I saw her smiling at my delight, and I shyly lowered the carton. "Thank you," I said.

I was not sure of how much soap to use, so I sprinkled a little of the white and bluish powder into my bucket of clothes and gave the carton back to her. She took the carton and added a generous amount to my bucket. My clothes felt slippery, and as I soon as I began to rub my clothes together, soapsuds started forming. It felt great to have my hands immersed in the wet, sudsy water and to breathe in the fresh smell of soap hanging in the air around me. When I got to her handkerchief, I took extra care to wash it thoroughly to remove all stains. I saw her staring at the handkerchief. I felt like I should say something.

"I will give it back to you after it dries," I told her.

"Keep it. It is a gift," she said.

I wondered if she had intended to give me the handkerchief as a gift yesterday when she gave it to me to wipe off the blood from my face. Maybe she was only saying that it was a gift now because I did not give it back sooner. Perhaps she thought I wanted to have it, and she was trying to help me save face by saying that it was a gift. Now I felt I must give her something in return, but I did not have anything.

"I cannot accept it," I said.

"Why not? Don't you like me?" Mayna asked.

Her directness caught me by surprise. I was confused and speechless. I could not figure out if her question was a simple invitation for friendship or if she was asking about something more. Her dark eyes were intense and probing as if she were trying to read an answer in my eyes. It was frustrating to be unable to speak normally to this girl. I had to choose my words carefully so as not to hurt her and not to be hurt by her.

"Uh . . . uh . . . I like you," I stammered. I could not believe I said it. The birds, the insects, the sound of children in the distance, and even the rustling of the leaves seemed to stand still as they and I waited for her reaction.

She smiled. "You keep the handkerchief."

Without really thinking, I reached inside the pocket of my pants and pulled out the smooth, iridescent marble that I found at Mr. Xiong's farm and offered it to her.

She accepted the marble and held it up to admire the colors. Then she looked at me and asked, "Are you sure you want me to have this?"

"Yes," I replied.

"Thank you."

She looked around as if she was checking to make sure everything was in place. Then she picked up her small basket of wet clothes and said that she had to go. As I watched her go, I was tempted to call her back so that I could talk to her some more, but I could not think of an excuse to give her for wanting her to stay. I just watched as she walked away. I wondered if she truly liked the marble or if she thought the marble was unworthy of her handkerchief, perhaps even childish. I wondered if she would chuck it as soon as she was out of my sight. Then she turned around. My heart skipped a beat.

"Blong!" she called.

"Yes," I replied trying not to sound too eager.

"I have not given you a bike ride yet. Do you still want a ride?"

Before I could pretend that it didn't really matter to me, an enthusiastic "yes" escaped my throat.

"Vameng has the bike right now, but I could use it tomorrow. Come by early tomorrow, and I'll take you for a ride."

I nodded at her, and she walked away.

Chapter 29

I could not wait until tomorrow, so I went to bed early that night. I had difficulty falling asleep, however. I kept thinking about the bike ride. I closed my eyes and pictured myself already knowing how to ride a bike. I pretended that I could ride a bike with no hands just like Vameng. I lifted my legs and made a circular motion like I was pedaling the bike fast. I imagined the wind blowing on my face as I pedaled faster and faster. Then Grandpa yelled at me to stop kicking the blanket.

I awoke the next morning before everyone else in my family. I did every chore that I thought Grandma might ask me to do that day so she would have no reason to keep me close by. I then went downstairs to see if Mayna was there, but she was nowhere in sight. Gosh! I hated waiting. I looked around for a few minutes. Perhaps I am too early, I thought. I went back upstairs. Then I wondered what if she came out earlier and did not see me like yesterday, and she was somewhere waiting for me. I rushed back downstairs and told myself I would stay in the open so that she could see me if she indeed was looking for me. I stood around and felt like a fool. I was close to giving up on her when I heard, "Hey, are you ready?"

I wanted to tell her I had been ready since last night, but I did not want to sound desperate.

"Ready for what?" I asked.

She looked at me perceptively and ignored my pretense at indifference.

"I saw you earlier, but I had to cook first," she explained. "Don't be mad at me. We will have fun today."

"I am not mad at you," I said, still trying to pretend I had not been waiting eagerly for her all morning.

"Let me go get the bike and tell my mom first," Mayna said and ran back to her house.

A few minutes later, she emerged from the house. She was pushing the bike and beckoned with her chin for me to go to her. I walked along as she continued to push the bike until we reached the road. She held the bike upright and said, "Get on. You can rest your feet there."

She pointed to the axle pegs on the back wheel. I climbed on the bike, sat as far back in the seat as I could, and rested my feet on the axle pegs.

"Now, once I climb on, put your hands on my shoulders only. Don't put your hands on my ribs. I am ticklish there. And don't grab me," she explained.

She swung her right leg over the bike to place her right foot on the pedal. Then she pushed off with her left foot and began pedaling. We started moving forward. The bike wobbled from side to side. I felt off balance like I was going to fall off, and I thought, "We are going to fall down again!"

"Put your hands on my shoulders!" she yelled.

I did not realize that I was grabbing her ribs, which was making her ticklish, and she was squirming to be free of my hands. I quickly put my hands on her shoulders. She slowly gained control of the bike, although it was still wobbly. She pedaled the bike standing up, which made it harder for me to keep my hold on her shoulders. She called out something about her waist.

"Huh?" I questioned.

"Put your hands on my waist so I could sit down," she ordered.

My grip on her shoulders was too tight, and I was unknowingly pulling her downward to sit on the center bar of the bike. I slid my hands down to her waist. She then hoisted herself up to sit comfortably on the front edge of the seat as she pedaled forward.

After we were steady, she called over her shoulder, "Do you like it?"

"Yes," I answered. Then I thought, did she mean the bike ride or holding her waist?

"It's not that bad, right?"

"Oh! Yes! I like the bike ride," I answered her.

There was a short pause. Then as if she read my mind, she questioned, "What did you think I was asking you about at first?"

I did not know what to say to her, so I just laughed. She did not laugh, but I could tell that she was smiling. I liked Mayna's long hair blowing in my face. I liked her voice too, which could be gentle and tender when she was nice, and commanding and harsh when she was bossy.

The bike was moving steadily now. I knew we had passed the corner of the street where we usually turned around to go back to the complex, but Mayna just kept going. I was puzzled.

"How come you are not turning around?"

"Why? You are the only one riding today," she replied.

"Are we going somewhere then?"

"You'll see."

She pedaled faster, her long hair floating in the air and brushing softly like feathers against my face. Her hair smelled nice, and I stealthily took in long whiffs of its fragrance. I felt like we were flying. Soon we were out in the country. We passed rice paddies. They stretched as far as the eyes could see. I wondered how strange that we were hoping to leave Laos, whereas many Laotians were planning for the days and years ahead. We rode past a fisherman coming back from a river. His little boy was proudly carrying a string of fish. We passed by farmers selling melons on the side of the road.

We traveled for quite some distance, and I could see that Mayna was getting tired. I wished I could help her. She gradually slowed down and then came to a stop.

"You can get down now," she told me.

I felt stupid for not knowing that. I got off the bike, and my behind felt sore from sitting. I walked slowly alongside her as she pushed the bike.

"You're walking funny," Mayna said with a smile.

"It was the seat."

"Is this your first time on a bike?"

"No, my first time was the other day."

She laughed. "I don't think we should count that time. We were hardly on the bike before we fell." Then she added, "You were terrible."

"Why was I terrible?"

"You grabbed me—where you were not supposed to!"

"I am sorry," I replied. "It was by mistake."

"I know," she said.

We walked in silence for a few minutes.

"Did you enjoy the ride?" asked Mayna.

"Yes, I felt like I was flying. How about you?"

"Yes, but I would enjoy it more if somebody knew how to pedal a bike so that I could just sit back," she teased.

I turned to look at her, and it happened that she had also turned to look at me. Everything seemed to be very still; even my heart seemed to have stopped beating. She gave me a huge smile as if to say that she was happy to be with me at that very moment. I smiled back at her, forgetting that I had crooked teeth. I wanted to reach out and touch her cheeks to see if they were as soft as they looked. Instead, I reached out and gently chucked her chin. She looked surprised, I looked surprised, and then I asked to push the bike. We walked on in silence.

Chapter 30

I was just thinking about how Mayna could make me so confused at times when she suddenly said, "Stop here" and took the bike from me. She pushed it to the edge of an area with tall grass. She set the bike on its side, and the bike disappearing into the thick grass. You could no longer tell that there was a bicycle hidden in there.

"What are you doing?" I asked.

She did not respond. She walked over to me and tagged me. "You're it!" She took off running along the edge of a rice paddy. I ran after her. She ran into a wooded area, and although I thought I was close behind, I soon lost sight of her. When I emerged from the wooded area, I was in a grove of fruit trees. The trees were evenly spaced apart as if they were planned. Each tree had plenty of exposure to sunlight. There were coconut, mango, orange, banana, guava, and papaya trees. Off to the side of the trees was a small tiki hut. There was a long bench that took up one side of the hut. I looked all over for her, but I could not find her. I called out her name, but there was no answer. I yelled that if she did not come out, I was going back home without her. Then a mango hit me on the head. I looked up and saw her in a tree, trying hard to suppress a giggle.

"Do you want some mangoes?" she yelled down.

"Yes, but I think they are still sour."

"So, we just eat them with salt and hot pepper."

"Did you pack salt and hot pepper?"

"No, but we have some in the hut. Go get them; they are in a jar hanging above the fire pit.

By the time I got back to the mango tree, she was on the ground. The front of her shirt was folded up like a bowl. There were mangoes inside. Their small size and oval shape made them look like green eggs. I set the salt and pepper down and went to tear off some clean banana leaves so we could put the mangoes on them. She poured a small amount of the salt and pepper mixture onto the banana leaves. Then she dipped the small end of a green mango into the salt and pepper mixture and took a loud bite. She crunched on the mango and made a funny face. My mouth started to water, and I joined her. One thing about sour mango with salt and pepper is once you eat it, you have to eat more and more. Soon my tongue was burning from the pepper, but I kept eating. I could tell she was suffering too from the pepper, but she was enjoying the taste too much to stop eating. We were perspiring, our eyes were watering, and our noses were running, but we were thoroughly enjoying the delicious, crunchy green mangoes with salt and pepper. To this day, and I am sure for the rest of life, whenever I see green mangoes, I will always think of Mayna and that afternoon.

"Do you have water?" I could hardly speak. My mouth was on fire.

"I don't know. Check the water jar over there." She pointed to the large ceramic jar at the corner of the hut.

The water jar was wider than I was, and the rim was just above my waist. I removed the cover and peered inside. I saw my reflection at the bottom in the darkness of the jar.

"There is still water, but it's low."

"The ladle should be in the bamboo basket."

The bamboo basket was hanging on a pole across the ceiling. I reached up and grabbed the ladle. I drank about five scoops of water, but my mouth was still burning. Mayna walked over, and I handed her the ladle.

"The pepper is hot," I commented.

"Yes," agreed Mayna. "My mouth is burning." She scooped some water to her mouth and drank rapidly.

"The water does not help," I said.

"I know, but I want some water anyway." Mayna scooped out some more water and quickly drank it down.

"How do I get rid of this burning?" I asked. My mouth hung open because the burning sensation on my tongue intensified whenever I closed my mouth.

"Bend over and open your mouth to let all the burning saliva drip out."

Mayna sat on the bench, dropped her head down between her knees, opened her mouth, and let the saliva drip out. I went to sit next to her and imitated her. After a little while, I could feel the burning starting to disappear. I lifted my head up and lay back on the bench. I stared at the ceiling made of wood and straw, and thought about the burning sensation in my mouth evaporating.

"How do you know this method of getting rid of the taste of hot peppers?" I asked.

"I learned it from my dad's Laotian friend."

There was silence as we lay there staring at the ceiling. The sun was shining brightly. An occasional breeze blew through the hut. Except for the sound of rustling leaves and tall grasses, all was silent. The overcrowding in the complex and the thought of escaping to Thailand seemed unreal now. Laos had peace and warm, breezy afternoons with which to pass the day. Surely, it must be just a bad dream that we were refugees trying to flee a war-torn country.

As if she was reading my thoughts and she did not want me to stray too far from reality, Mayna said matter-of-factly, "You know, a family on the second floor is moving back. They are not going to flee the country anymore. Maybe you and your grandparents can move into their room."

"What?" I asked, trying to make sense of what Mayna had just said as I came back from my revelries.

"A family at the complex is going back. I was thinking that maybe you and your family could move into their room since all of you sleep on the balcony."

"How do you know they are moving back?"

"The other day they asked my brother to go and buy some food for them. They told him that they didn't have enough money to take them to Thailand."

"I feel bad for them. They have come so far," I said and thought about how far we were from Long Cheng.

"I know," Mayna said forlornly.

"Are you sad?" I asked.

"It is just that all my friends are leaving for Thailand. I know soon you will be leaving too."

"Will you and your family eventually leave?" I asked.

"No. My dad keeps saying that we have lots of cows, buffalo, and rice fields here. He does not want to leave everything behind. People keep leaving, and he keeps buying all their things. I will never escape Laos. I am terrified of what the future holds for my family and me. After all the victory celebrations, the new government will want to settle scores and determine who stands where. My father did not fight in the war. He is a businessman and a farmer, not a soldier, but we are Hmong."

I did not know how to comfort her, so I just listened.

"There used to be a lot of farmers around here. They were our friends, both Lao and Hmong. Coming to the farm was fun even though it was hard work. There were some afternoons when we would take a break from farming to catch fish. That was fun. Now hardly anyone comes here except our family and some Laotian families. Most of them are strangers. We don't know them," explained Mayna. "And in school," she added, "I used to have many friends, but now . . ." Then abruptly she changed the subject. "Let's go back to town."

We walked back to the bike. She seemed different from the happy girl earlier. I guessed we all had our own sadness and fear because of the war, our future uncertain and our lives in suspension. But her fear of what might happen after the victory celebrations filled me with dread. There did

141

seem to be a kind of surreal calm in the land, the kind of calm that usually precedes a storm.

Several years later as the situation in Laos worsened, horrific stories emerged that young Hmong girls were forced to entertain Communist soldiers, Hmong men were rounded up and sent to "re-education" camps, and little Hmong children were maimed by the Communists in public squares as punishment for their parents' noncompliance or involvement in helping the United States CIA. Communist soldiers also open-fired on any Hmong crossing the Mekong River, trying to reach Thailand. The new Communist government seemed determined to punish the Hmong and needed no substantial, legitimate reason. The Communists were highly outraged and insulted that the Hmong, whom they saw as at the bottom of society, living on the fringe, dared to aid America, an enemy.

As I listened to those stories, Mayna's plaintive words came back to me. I found myself praying and hoping that she was safe. I often wondered about her and whether she and her family came to America. At Hmong New Year celebrations and soccer tournaments, I sometimes found myself scanning the crowd for her, hoping that by some chance she came to America. One time while grabbing a slice of pizza and pop between classes, I saw a girl who, for a moment, I thought was her.

Chapter 31

Grandma woke me up early like she did almost every morning, shouting and hollering.

"Wake up! Wake up! The sun is already up. Wake up!"

I was tired and still wanted to sleep, but I did not want Grandma yelling in my ear, so I slowly got up.

"Here is the bucket. Go wash up and fetch me some water so I can make food to feed your grandfather and you."

I took the bucket from Grandma and stumbled downstairs. I was halfway downstairs when Grandma called out to me. I turned around to listen to her.

"When you come back, don't forget to stop by Mr. Thao's house and ask to see if his son could go and buy some meat for your grandfather."

I turned around and walked back downstairs, too tired to answer her. I wondered why Grandma always made it sound like Grandpa and I were the only two people who ate. I washed myself quietly at the well and filled my bucket with water. On my way back, I stopped by Mr. Thao's house. I hesitated because Mr. Thao was Mayna's father. I raised a fist and was just about to knock on the door when it suddenly opened. Then Mayna was standing in front of me.

"I was wondering how much longer it would be before you knocked on the door," she said, her eyes twinkling, and I knew she had been watching me from inside her house.

"Is your dad home?" I asked.

"Yes, what do you want him for?"

"My grandma wanted me to ask your dad to see if your brother Vameng could go to the morning market and buy some meat for my grandpa."

"I will take you there," Mayna answered.

"Aren't you supposed to ask your dad for permission first?"

"Okay." She closed the door on me. Minutes later she opened the door and said, "Let's go."

"Did you ask your dad?" I questioned her.

"Oh yes, my mom said I could take you."

"Okay, I did not know that we have to go right away. Let me take this bucket of water to my grandma first. But I'm not sure if she will let me go or not."

"She has to let you go. We are taking the bike, and you need to watch the bike while I shop. Tell her that."

I was excited about going to the morning market. I had heard other kids say the morning market in Vientiane was huge. The water in the bucket sloshed about as I hastily climbed the stairs. Mayna watched until I reached the second story, then she left to go get the bike. I suddenly felt stupid and realized Grandma would not need the water upstairs, but I was almost at the top, so I carried the bucket all the way to the third floor as if that was my intention in the first place. Grandma gave me a perplexed look when she saw me and asked, "Why did you bring the bucket of water up here?"

"I thought you might want to wash your face up here." I was playing dumb with her.

"I have already washed. You know better. Take the water downstairs to the cooking area," ordered Grandma, annoyed at my stupidity.

I could not believe it myself that a girl could make me do crazy, brainless things. I felt absent-minded whenever Mayna was around. Before going downstairs, I said, "Grandma, Mr. Thao's daughter could buy the meat for us, but she . . . she wants me to go with her to watch the bike while she shops."

Grandma gave me a look like she did not quite believe me. Then she turned her back to me and dug under the front part of her belt for a small cloth bag that was hidden in the folds of her Laotian skirt and held in place by the belt. It was some time before she finally pulled out the bag. Grandma was not one to part with her money easily. She slowly counted out each bill. She knew the value of each bill not by the numbers printed on them but by the pictures on the money. Although Grandma did not know how to read or write, she knew her money. "Here are fifty kips. I want you to get meat, salt, mustard greens, and three eggs."

I accepted the money from her. "Grandma, I don't think this is enough money to buy all you are asking for."

Grandma looked at me. She seemed indecisive. Finally, she said, "Don't buy the mustard greens then."

It was pointless to explain to Grandma the cost of things, so I went downstairs. I decided that I would ask Mayna to buy only meat and salt. The money was too little, and I knew it was not going to be enough for the eggs. When I returned, I would tell Grandma that the money was just enough to buy meat and salt. Mayna was already waiting with the bike when I reached downstairs. She pushed the bike and walked along with me as I carried the bucket of water to the cooking area. The water inside sloshed about and splashed my legs as I quickened my steps. A smile tugged at the corner of Mayna's lips.

Soon we were off. She did not struggle with the bike this time. Either I knew how to center myself now, or she just got better at handling the bike with a passenger. The road to the market was desolate since all the vendors and farmers were already at the market. With the cool morning breeze on my face and the speed of the bike, I felt like I was flying. Sometimes when the road was flat, I closed my eyes, let go of my hold on Mayna and spread out my arms. The feeling was exhilarating. We passed by some of the most beautiful temples and monuments I had ever seen. They appeared small in the distance and then loomed up as we approached.

When we reached the market, the road was congested with cars, songthaews, bicycles, and pedestrians. Even the air was congested with all sorts of noises—cars honking, bicycle bells tinkling, friends and relatives exclaiming delighted greetings to one another, vendors calling out to no one in particular the excellent quality of their merchandises or the deliciousness of their food, and Laotian music blaring from everywhere. The savory smell of noodles and fried meat permeated the air, making my stomach growl for whatever was steaming, boiling, grilling, or sizzling nearby. The market was vibrant, pulsating with a multitude of things to see, hear, touch, taste, and smell. All my senses were overwhelmed.

The thick crowd made it impossible for Mayna to control the bike. We got off the bike, and she pushed it while we walked past the food vendors. I knew the money Grandma gave me was not going to be enough for the grocery items, let alone a bowl of noodles, so I was a little embarrassed that Mayna and I were passing through this section. What if she was hoping I would treat her to a bowl of noodles or something?

I tried not to openly stare at the steaming pots of noodles, the golden-brown roasted chicken thighs and pork ribs, the piles of soft and steaming crepes filled with ground pork and green onions, and all the other goodies that were hot, delicious, and tempting. The smells of all those delicious foods were intoxicating! I could smell the pungent fish sauce and garlic of a papaya salad before I saw a vendor busily mixing it in a mortar and pounding it down with a pestle. The smell of spicy curry and coconut teased my nostrils before I saw a vendor ladling curry soup over a bowl of soft white noodles topped with shredded cabbage, cilantro, and mint. The fragrant smell of freshly steamed rice and sizzling pork floated to me, and I could imagine biting into the warm, fluffy rice and smoky pork. I wished I had money, and if I did, I would buy one thing from each vendor and taste everything. What torture it was to be among such tantalizing food and to be so utterly broke.

"Blong, let me do all the talking, okay?" Then as if she realized I might be confused, she continued in a lowered voice, "I don't want to draw too much attention to us being Hmong."

"Okay," I replied, but my mind was more on the food than on what she was saying. Suddenly, Mayna motioned her head toward the military soldiers who were walking around. That jolted me from my food fantasy.

"Those soldiers are probably looking for Hmong people who are trying to escape Laos," said Mayna angrily.

"Yes," I replied and felt fear rising in me. The morning market was bustling with people who were loud and friendly and who shouted instead of talked. Those soldiers ruined the happy energy of the place.

"I'm hungry. Let's stop at the older lady over there's stall and have some noodles and papaya salad. She makes the best papaya salad," said Mayna. There was a note of authority in her voice. Mayna's air of familiarity with the market was comforting. The nearby soldiers seemed less intimidating, and I felt as if somehow everything would be all right.

"I did not bring my money today," I lied to her. Then quickly I added, "I only have Grandma's grocery money."

"That's okay. I will treat you. You are going to love the papaya salad!" Money seemed not to be an issue at all with her.

I felt embarrassed because Mayna probably knew I was hungry by the way I stole glances at all the food on display.

"I'm really not hungry, you know. I can watch the bike while you eat." I said those words, yet I was already salivating at the thought of noodles and papaya salad.

"You think just because we live in Vientiane, my parents did not raise me with any manners?" She smiled and gently punched my right arm. "Even in Vientiane, we do not let our friends just watch us eat. C'mon, eat with me. I am

147

convinced you have never tasted papaya salad this good where you came from."

"Thank you," I muttered, although I felt there was something more I wanted to say but could not put into words. Years later, I realized that what I wanted to say to her on that day was that I was deeply grateful to her, not just for the food but for her generosity, kindness, and friendship. She made me feel that it was my company she wanted, not a charity case to make her feel good about herself.

She gave me a smile that showed she was pleased that I was not going to continue backing out of eating with her.

"What kind of noodles would you like?" she asked.

"I don't know," I replied, feeling a bit overwhelmed and eager at the same time. "I will have whatever you have."

"No, you have to have something different so we can sample each other's noodles," explained Mayna.

"What if my noodles don't taste good?"

"You cannot go wrong here. All the noodles are good!"

"I want a bowl of beef pho."

"Then I will have a bowl of kapoon," said Mayna. "How many peppers can you handle in papaya salad?"

"I can handle four peppers." Then I thought four might be too spicy for her.

She gave me a look of disbelief. "Four peppers? You won't be able to taste the peppers. I thought where you came from, Hmong people ate spicy food. What about seven peppers?"

She was daring me! I ate peppers all my life. I could handle more than seven peppers. "I can handle eight," I told her.

"Let's make it ten then," said Mayna.

"All right then," I agreed with her. We both knew the papaya salad was going to be too hot, but neither of us wanted to be the one to back down. The green mangoes and peppers burning our tongues just a few days ago were no longer on our minds.

We walked up to the Laotian lady and waited for an open seat. She saw Mayna and beckoned to her. She pulled out two stools and set them at the end of the table and pointed for us to sit there. We pushed the bike to the back of the stall and leaned it against a wooden pole where we could see the bike from our sitting area. Mayna spoke Lao very well and chatted with the Laotian lady as the lady prepared noodles for other customers. Mayna ordered a bowl of pho, a bowl of kapoon, and papaya salad with ten peppers. The Laotian lady looked at us like we were crazy and asked Mayna again if we really wanted ten peppers. Mayna told her yes.

The papaya salad was served with long-stemmed greens with triangular leaves. We both stared at the mound of creamy-white papaya shreds. The red bits of crushed chili peppers in the salad looked intimidating, but the smell of garlic, fish sauce, and lime made my mouth water, and I wanted to help myself to some papaya salad even though I knew it would be extremely spicy. Mayna broke off a leaf from the greens and used it to pinch a generous amount of papaya salad and put it in her mouth. "Mmm." She momentarily closed her eyes in satisfaction.

I stabbed the top of the papaya salad mound with my fork and brought a dripping heap into my mouth. All at once my taste buds were assaulted with the flavors of salty fish sauce, pungent garlic, tangy lime, roasted peanuts, and hot, fiery peppers. The papaya salad was excellent! We ate, drank water, blew our noses, and ate again. By the time the bowls of noodles were ready, we had already cleaned up the plate of papaya salad. We even tilted the plate and drank up the hot papaya juice.

Mayna's bowl of kapoon came with all the ingredients already in it, whereas my bowl of pho came with a small plate of herbs, bean sprouts, and lime wedges. In the center of the table were several bottles of sauces for the pho. I put some herbs and bean sprouts into my bowl and squeezed in some lime juice, but the bottles of sauces were far for my reach. I waited a few minutes, hoping that the Laotian lady would see that I needed the condiments and move them closer to me, but she was busy serving other customers. I tried a spoonful of my broth. It tasted good but not full-bodied, not spicy, and not satisfying. The sauces would really improve the flavor of the broth. That is how pho is supposed to be eaten. You have a seasoned beef broth as a base, and then you add sauces and herbs to your own bowl to suit your individual taste. I did not want to ask the Laotian lady to pass me the sauces because I did not speak Lao well, and Mayna had told me not to speak because my Hmong accent might draw unwanted attention.

I ate my noodles slowly, hoping that Mayna would notice that I needed the sauces. After a few hungry, rapid bites of her kapoon, Mayna finally looked up and saw that my pho looked plain; the broth was still clear. She gave me a perplexed look, pushed her bowl toward me, and then took mine. She tasted a spoonful of the pho soup and made a face. "This is bland. It is good if you are feeding a baby, but don't you want more flavor than this?" Without waiting for my reply, she asked the Laotian lady for the bottles of sauces and began shaking different sauces into my bowl. I tasted her kapoon. It was good, but I preferred pho. I pushed her bowl back to her, and she pushed my bowl back to me. I ate my bowl of noodles with all the pho condiments that Mayna had put in. Surprisingly, she had seasoned it exactly the way I liked it. When we were done eating, Mayna paid the Laotian lady and asked her to look after the bike while we shop for groceries.

We went to the meat section first. On large tables, there were whole chickens, cut-up pieces of chicken, different cuts of pork and beef, fish, and above the meats, flies hovered and buzzed.

"I thought you said you weren't hungry," Mayna teased, referring to how fast I ate my bowl of noodles. I smiled, and she added, "I hope you didn't mind that I put sauces in your pho."

"No, actually I wanted to put some in, but you told me not to speak, and the sauces were too far for me to reach."

"Really? Did you still like the bowl of pho after I put the sauces in?"

"No," I replied and tried to look disappointed.

She stopped to look at me and realized I was only teasing her. She lightly punched me on the arm. We walked down a few rows where the butchers were calling out claims that they had the best meats. We stopped at one of the stalls, and Mayna started haggling with the butcher. She took on the mannerism and speaking tone of the Laotian ladies around her. I watched in amazement at her transformation. If it were me, I would just pay whatever price the butcher wanted. After several minutes, she was able to convince the butcher to lower the price. We bought some pork, but we did not have enough money to buy anything else. I was thrilled, however. With such a large hunk of pork, maybe Grandma could fry it up for Grandpa and her.

We walked back to get her bike from the noodle stall. The Laotian lady was busy with customers, but she smiled at us. Between ladling steaming broth over bowls of noodles and handing the bowls to customers, the Laotian lady carried on a conversation with Mayna. After Mayna told her that I had just a little bit of money left but still needed to buy salt for my grandma, the Laotian lady gave me a small bag of salt for the remaining money that I had. We thanked her and said goodbye. Like an affectionate aunt, she told Mayna to come back and see her again soon.

We got our bike and rode back to the complex. A few soldiers stared at us, but Mayna kind of looked Laotian. In fact, many Hmong people in the complex thought she was Laotian. One time a Hmong lady asked Mayna's mom if she had adopted "a Laotian girl" because she had all sons and no daughter. Mrs. Thao yelled at the lady, "Laotian girl? What Laotian girl? My Mayna is my daughter. She came from my womb!"

When we got back to the complex, I thanked Mayna and went to the cooking area. Grandma and some other ladies were busily preparing meals for their families. Because everybody in the complex cooked in the same area, the clay stoves were on a first-come-first-served basis. Some families were already finished eating and some, like mine, were still cooking. I gave her the salt and pork. I thought she would be pleased by the size of the pork, which I was able to get only because of Mayna's excellent haggling skills. Grandma unwrapped the meat and the salt and said, "Where are the vegetables and eggs?"

"Grandma, meat is very expensive now. This is all. With the money you gave me, this was all I could buy."

Grandma looked like she did not believe me until the lady next to her said, "For fifty kips, you did well. This is what I got for seventy-five kips." She showed her package of meat to Grandma, which was smaller than what Mayna and I got.

Grandma ignored her and asked, "Where is the change?"

"Grandma, we used all the change to buy salt."

"Hmm. You should have bought a smaller cut of meat and some vegetables. We are humble people. We should not eat meat without vegetables. What will other people think of us?" Grandma always used meat sparingly so that it would just flavor a dish and not become the dish.

I was frustrated with Grandma. She always did this. She would give whoever was going to the market so little money to buy so much, and sometimes when the person came back with only a few of the items, she would peel off a few more bills or count out a few more coins and ask that person to go back for the rest of the items.

Chapter 32

The days were once again endless and boring. Every day was the same: I woke up, packed my clothes, sat around with nothing to do until noon, ate whatever Grandma made for lunch, sat around with nothing to do again until supper, and then unpacked my things. How I wish we could go to Thailand. Things would not be so dull if I could go outside and play. I had not been outside for two weeks now. All the other kids had been cooped up in their apartments too, so I should not complain. Uncle Kou told Grandpa to make sure I didn't leave the complex and that I could only go out for necessary reasons.

A Hmong man had been taken away by the authorities. Several weeks had passed, and still, nobody knew of his whereabouts. Mr. Thao was extremely worried and frightened. He did not want us children to play outside anymore.

I was sitting on the balcony with my legs dangling over the edge, hoping to see Mayna come out to go fetch water from the well or out to do some sort of chore for her mother. Suddenly a pair of hands gripped my shoulders and pushed me forward slightly. I screamed and quickly turned around. It was Uncle Kou. He pulled me back again to him and laughed. He tousled my hair and sat down next to me.

"What are you doing?" he asked.

"Nothing."

"You like the little girl down there?" teased Uncle Kou, pointing to Mayna's house.

"No," I quickly denied.

"Well, then you might have a problem 'cause I think she likes you."

"I don't like her," I said a little too quickly. Uncle Kou just smiled at me like he knew something I did not.

"Where is your grandma?" Uncle Kou changed the subject.

"I don't know. Maybe she went down to get the fire ready."

"Go get your grandma," ordered Uncle Kou. "You and Grandma are going to Thailand."

I could not believe it! I excitedly ran down the stairs. I was going to see my sister, my cousins, and my aunts and uncles again, I thought. Some people in the complex stuck their heads out to see what was going on. I could hear some of the older tenants shouting for me to not make so much noise. When I reached Grandma, I was short of breath and could hardly speak.

"Grandma! Grandma! Uncle Kou said for you to get ready. We are going to Thailand."

Grandma dropped the firewood she was carrying. Tears welled up in her eyes and rolled down her cheeks. I didn't know if she was happy or sad. Grandma walked quickly upstairs, and I followed her. When we reached our corner of the balcony, we saw that Grandpa and Uncle Kou were talking. Uncle Kou looked up at us and beckoned for us to move closer.

"Mom," he addressed Grandma, "Dad and I decided that it will be just you and Blong going to Thailand. Dad and I will come at a later time. Security is tight. It is better for you and Blong to go without Dad because soldiers will not expect you and Blong to cross without a man."

"But I don't know the Thai Language, and I know just a little bit of Lao. I'm afraid," said Grandma.

"Don't worry. I have made arrangements with Miss Monkey so that you do not have to speak any Lao on the Laotian side, and once you get to Thailand, there will be Thai people waiting to take you to the refugee camp. When you get to the camp, ask for Nhia Tong Yang."

I remembered Uncle Nhia Tong. I had not thought about him in a while, but the mentioning of his name

154

instantly brought back memories of his sons whom I had played with. I was glad that he was already in Thailand. He was a soft-spoken man who commanded respect without demanding it. I knew he would help us once we got there. I was not so sure about Miss Monkey, though. I was not very confident that a monkey could arrange things and help us. Actually, I was terrified of monkeys.

"Dad knows Lao well, and it will be easier for him to escape without you and Blong. Miss Monkey will be here soon, so pack what you need." Uncle Kou looked at Grandma and added, "Just pack your clothes and nothing else."

Grandma looked at me with fear, and I told her not to be afraid even though I was. Over the past few months, we had heard more stories about how Laotian boatmen would take Hmong refugees to the middle of the Mekong River and then demand more money. If the Hmong refugees did not give them more money, the boatmen would tip the boat over to drown them.

After checking around to make sure she was not leaving anything valuable behind, Grandma gathered her things and descended the stairs. Some people waved goodbye to us and said words of good luck and encouragement to Grandma. Others looked at us with worried expressions.

I saw Mayna standing in the doorway of her house. She was leaning against one side of the doorway. Her smile that I had grown to love was not there. She was staring at me with a sad expression. I remembered how empty Ka-Ying and I felt at the farm when we found out that the Xiongs had left for Thailand. I waved a reluctant goodbye to her. She raised her hand halfway and waved back. Then her hand dropped to her cheeks, and she began wiping away tears with the back of her hand.

Uncle Kou, Grandma, and I walked toward the street. There was a car waiting for us. Inside were a Laotian man and a Laotian lady. The lady was dressed in a red outfit. I looked around for the monkey but did not see one.

"Where is Miss Monkey?" I asked.

Grandma cut her eyes at me and told me to stop speaking nonsense. I was a little hurt by her abruptness and irritation. I thoroughly scanned the inside of the car one more time, looking for a small monkey since a big one would be visible by now. Grandma gave me an angry look and pointed her chin at the Laotian lady. I finally got it. The word "red" and the word "monkey" are homophones in the Hmong language. I realized that the Laotian lady was referred to as Miss Red because she was dressed in red. There was no monkey.

"Who is he?" Uncle Kou asked in Lao, referring to the man.

"He's my cousin and my driver," answered Miss Red.

We climbed into the car. I turned to look at the building complex for the last time. Mayna had advanced from her doorway as if she were coming to say goodbye but then changed her mind. She was now standing in the full sunshine and not in the shadow of her doorway. I was thankful for a clear, final view of her. Our eyes locked, and we said our silent goodbyes.

As the car pulled away, some of the boys from the complex started chasing the car and waving goodbye like we always did when one of us left. To my surprise, Mayna suddenly broke into a run with the boys. Then either she was a faster runner than the boys or the boys slowed down, for she quickly overtook them and was so close to the car that if I reached out, I could touch her outstretched hand. But before I could act, the car switched gear and pulled away. Mayna slowed down to stand staring at us, her hands on her hips and her chest heaving from trying to catch her breath. I waved to her, but she did not wave back. I watched the dust from the car swirl behind us, blocking my view of her.

We drove on the same street that Mayna and I rode her bike on when we went to the morning market. I saw two children riding a bicycle. The sight sent a pang through my heart. Seemed like it was just yesterday that Mayna and I were having fun, and today I did not even have time to say a proper farewell to her.

When we reached the boat station, Miss Red handed Grandma a bundle, which was a Laotian outfit, and told her to change into it right there in the car. The clothes were big enough that Grandma could easily put them on over her own clothes. She now looked like a Laotian lady, I thought. Miss Red then put a hat on my head to cover the bad haircut that Grandpa gave me. I was mad at Grandpa for giving me a bad haircut, but Grandpa and Grandma insisted that it was a good haircut. I was glad that Miss Red covered it up.

The street to the ticket booth was filled with vendors. They were selling all kinds of things. One vendor was selling large, straw sun hats. Nearby was a large boat, filling up with people, but we knew that the boat would not leave until it was full. We started to approach the ticket counter and then noticed the back of a soldier standing close by. Everywhere we looked, there seemed to be soldiers. We stopped and pretended to look at some of the things that the street vendors were selling. We wandered back and forth, hoping the soldiers would leave. Instead, more soldiers arrived. They looked solemn and menacing in their dark green uniforms. The soldiers walked in pairs, and now two were approaching the vendors' area. Four soldiers were checking the passengers on the boat and talking to them.

One of the soldiers looked straight at Grandma and me and then started walking briskly toward us. I was terrified; I just froze there not knowing what to do. By the time I got myself together, Grandma was gone. I panicked. The soldier kept walking toward me. He was getting closer. I thought of running, but I could visualize all the soldiers chasing after me and shooting me down. He was just a few yards from me now. Then someone called out to him. He turned around to see who it was. Right at that moment someone grabbed me and pulled me behind a small group of people in the back of a stall. A car pulled up in front of us, and I was shoved into the car. Grandma was already in there. I knew I was safe.

Miss Red was the person who shoved me into the car. She was wearing a large straw hat now like the ones I saw earlier. She pushed me lower into the seat. We drove away, and I could see the soldier's confused expression as he scanned the crowd for me. Miss Red pulled the big hat off her head and put it against the car window to shield us as we drove past the soldier.

We drove for a long time back and forth along the Mekong River. We drove past the boat station several times; each time we looked longingly at it. The boat station was so close, yet soldiers were about. We finally drove away and stopped at a house that was a good mile away from the boat station. Miss Red got out and went inside the house. The driver continued driving us around. I looked at Grandma. Her pale face sagged, and her eyes were closed. I knew she was becoming carsick. She looked like she was going to vomit any minute now. Luckily, just then we arrived in front of the house where we had dropped Miss Red off earlier. She came rushing out and hurried us into the house. After what seemed like just a moment's wait, she rushed us out the back.

The backyard was on a cliff overlooking the Mekong River. Grandma and I suddenly found ourselves staring down at the wide, yellow river. We didn't know it then, but that river would become the watery grave of many Hmong refugees to come. At Miss Red's insistence, we descended steep stairs that led down to the water's edge. A longtail boat was waiting for us, and Grandma stared wide-eyed at it.

From her expression, I knew that terror was building up inside of her like before. I prayed that she would not refuse to get in the boat this time. We were fortunate to have this second chance. She was probably wondering how was this long, slender boat going to take us safely across the Mekong River. The Laotian boatman also looked rough and unfriendly. I was terrified of him; Grandma looked terrified of him. But we must not let this chance slip away.

Thank goodness, Miss Red took charge. She hastened us to step into the boat. The boat rocked slightly as I stepped onboard. I quickly moved to sit close to the boatman. I gripped the sides of the narrow boat while Grandma gingerly stepped inside. She bent over and held on to one side of the boat as she slowly made her way to me. Her movement caused the boat to tilt slightly to one side, which made me more nervous.

As soon as she sat down, the boatman pulled on the cable to start the engine. The engine sputtered and then died. He pulled the cable again, but the engine did not even make a noise the second time. He pulled it with more force, and the boat rocked from the force of the pull. Grandma screamed out to me that he was going to drown us. He motioned to her to not scream, but Grandma screamed anyway. She screamed, cried, prayed, and called for our ancestors to help us. The boatman looked exasperated and worried, probably afraid that neighbors might hear Grandma. He ignored her and focused his attention on vigorously pulling the rope in rapid successions. The boat swayed from side to side. Some water splashed into the boat.

Finally, the engine revved up. With a relieved and frustrated glance at Grandma, he sped us away. My back was toward Thailand. As we moved farther and farther away from Laos, I could see the Laotian side getting smaller. I could see Miss Red climbing the stairs, making her way back up to the house, and then the stairs becoming smaller and smaller until they disappeared into the side of the cliff. Soon I could not even tell which house we came out of. I turned to face the front. The sun was low on the horizon. The fading light made the yellow river look opaque. I tried not to think about the terrifying expanse of the wide river and the notion that if I fell overboard, my body would be lost forever, never to be found in this murky water.

I watched as the Thai shoreline came into focus; the general greenery was transforming into trees. We were close to shore. All the anticipation, excitement, and fear I felt earlier were dissipating. I wondered if I was going to see my sister that evening and if I was going to have a nice meal and a warm place to sleep.

I thought about Mayna. I wondered what she was doing at that very moment. Maybe she was fetching water from the well to start the evening meal. How lonesome she must be: a solitary figure in the evening carrying water from the well. I thought again of our trip to the countryside and what she had said about being left behind. I felt empty. I knew too well the fear and panic of being left behind. The emptiness swelled into a heavy, painful ache in my chest even though this time I was the one leaving Laos.

Author's Note

As an English major and history minor, I have always been intrigued by the intersection of history and literature. Not only does literature attempt to fill in the gaps left by history, but, for me, literature packages complex issues into something that is easier to process. Some of the best historians I know had no formal education, yet their recollection of events, analysis, and presentation are more compelling than anything written. These people are the aunties, uncles, grandparents, and houseguests of my childhood.

I chose to set this story in the time right after the fall of Laos to Communism, which was the same year that the Vietnam War ended. Although the wind of change was starting to blow, the victors were temporarily preoccupied. This was before the genocide of the Hmong and the re-education camps in Laos.

My family's journey out of Laos took careful planning and precaution, but it was nowhere as horrific as that of other Hmong families afterwards. Of course, I was a child, and my recollection is through a child's memory distorted by the years.

I vaguely remember jumping off a cliff into a boat. However, my mother tells a different story. She said that in the chaos of boarding the boats, I was almost left behind. She said everyone was in the boats and the engine had started when she saw that I was not in the other boat with my father. I was, in her words, standing on the riverbank looking bewildered and cute in my little red dress. She screamed. My father jumped out of the boat onto the riverbank, swooped me up, and jumped back into the boat seconds before it sped off.

About the Author

May Y. Yang has a B.A. in English and an M.Ed in English Education from the University of Minnesota. She taught high school English for six years in St. Paul. Then she and her family moved to Florida, where she taught for twelve years, one year in Orlando and eleven years in Winter Haven.

"Growing up North in an urban setting, I never thought I would feel so completely welcomed and comfortable in a Southern town although my students had never even heard of the Hmong," she said. Family reasons made her decide to return home to Minnesota. She taught for one year in Minneapolis.

Yang currently lives in Brooklyn Park, Minnesota, where it is a short drive to Hmong flea markets in St. Paul. She once asked her mother if the Hmong flea markets were like the morning markets in Laos. "Not even close, my daughter," her mother replied.

Yang began writing *Leaving Laos* when she first moved to Florida. She worked on it on and off throughout the years. When she returned to Minnesota, she happened to watch a PBS documentary about the Secret War in Laos. There was a scene that brought her to tears. After a good, long cry, she decided to finish writing her book.

What Yang treasures most is her relationship with her family and friends. She is grateful for the love, support, and wisdom of family and friends in Minnesota, Florida, and other places.

Please visit Yang's website: **www.mayyangbooks.com**. She would love to hear from you.

Thank you for reading this book. If you enjoyed it, please consider leaving a review at the site where you purchased it. Word of mouth is crucial to the success of any writer.

Made in United States
North Haven, CT
02 March 2023

33401714R00102